Daybook from Sheep Meadow

Daybook from Sheep Meadow

The Notebooks of Tallis Martinson

Peter Dimock

Deep Vellum Publishing
Dallas, Texas

Deep Vellum Publishing
3000 Commerce St., Dallas, Texas 75226
deepvellum.org · @deepvellum

Deep Vellum is a 501c3 nonprofit literary arts organization
founded in 2013 with the mission to bring
the world into conversation through literature.

Support for this publication has been provided in part by a grant from
the City of Dallas Office of Arts and Culture's ArtsActivate program.

ISBNs: 978-1-64605-059-8 (paperback) | 978-1-64605-060-4 (ebook)

LIBRARY OF CONGRESS CONTROL NUMBER: 2021933576

Front cover design by Justin Childress | justinchildress.co

Interior Layout and Typesetting by KGT

Printed in the United States of America

For Ariana

INTRODUCTION

Learning to Practice
My Brother's Method

*A broken going on being for which there is remedy in speech
offered in air to welcome the immediacy of another's infinite
value.*

　　　　　—From the first entry in the Notebooks of
Tallis Martinson, dated Monday, November 3, 2003

I DECIDED TO LEARN TO practice my brother's method
after I found three entries from his notebooks transcribed
onto a folded and frayed sheet of ordinary typing paper.
The folded white sheet lay loose inside one of the three
boxes that held all 126 of his handwritten notebooks.

I still often recite these entries to myself from
memory:

April 28, 2004

—This use of time—water over stones—the sound of
it, as if this were victory—an overturning, an uncover-
ing—this catastrophe, this action—a gesture—restraining

apocalypse—for the ear there is never an end to hearing; for the eye, never an end to seeing—now is the time for order and for carrying children in our hearts like words— for speech in a landscape in which the painted bird sings, then flies. [I.1; II.1; III.1a–1b; IV.1; V.1]

November 7, 2004

—Sweetness in the bone—a new kind of light—this failure of democracy and the success of empire—a lust past all possession fulfilled in light—a violence no one wanted to survive—an ecstasy of unanswerable force past every betrayed possibility of reciprocity. I felt my thought and ordinary ecstatic American perception become one. [I.2; II.1; III.2a–2b; IV.2; V.2]

April 2, 2005

—For meditations on historical justice it is helpful to memorize verbatim the following strict, formal definition of language and keep it refreshed in the mind so that it is always ready for spontaneous use: "Language is a combinatorial system capable of generating an unbounded number of creative expressions interpretable at two interfaces: the cognitive/intentional and the sensorimotor (roughly thought and sound)." [I.3; II.1; III.3a–3b; IV.3; V.3]

In the late fall of 2015, my brother, the respected American historian Tallis Martinson, left instructions that the boxes holding his notebooks be placed in my custody and be made subject to my editorial control during his residency in the mental hospital to which he voluntarily committed himself. The facility's name is Lakehill Long-Term Psychiatric Care. It is located in upstate New York. Tallis's instructions specified further that all his unpublished writings were to be put in my possession and under my editorial control in the event of his death. Beneath the folded piece of paper with the notebook entries lay another loose page on which Tallis had typed what appeared to be journalists' brief summaries, in chronological order, of several events from the Iraq War. The first three events bore dates corresponding to the dates of the notebook entries. I present these documents and their circumstances to introduce the reader of these initial selections from my brother's notebooks to the sound created in the mind by what Tallis called his "entirely new method for enacting historical justice."

April 28, 2004	First airing by CBS of report documenting systematic torture by US personnel of Iraqi prisoners at Abu Ghraib.
November 7, 2004	The Second Battle of Fallujah begins and lasts until December 23
April 2, 2005	Battle of Abu Ghraib prison
April 5, 2010	Release of gunsight footage from

	July 12, 2007, of an air-to-ground attack by two US AH-64 Apache helicopters in Baghdad that killed seven unarmed men, including two journalists, and severely wounded two children
April 18, 2010	Iraqi Special Operations Forces kill ISIL's leadership, Abu Ayyub al-Masri and Abu Omar al-Baghdadi. A US Black Hawk UH-60 helicopter supporting the operation crashes, killing a Ranger sergeant and injuring the aircrew
August 2, 2010	*The New York Times* announces partial withdrawal of US troops
August 18, 2010	The official end of US effective combat operations in Iraq
August 19, 2010	Operation Iraqi Freedom officially ends
November 4, 2010	Ayman al-Zawahiri threatens new attacks on the US
January 27, 2012	A suicide bomber in Baghdad kills 33 people and wounds 65 others

August 16, 2012	A series of bombings kills more than 90 people across Iraq
March 2, 2015	Coalition of Iraqi Armed Forces and militia numbering around 30,000 launch an offensive against Islamic State positions in Tikrit

Tallis's first notebook entry is dated November 3, 2003; the last is dated April 5, 2015. On April 28, 2010, Tallis gave sworn testimony as an expert witness before a House sub-committee hearing on the legality of the use of armed drones by US armed forces and government personnel for targeted assassinations beyond an active battlefield. He was invited to testify by the committee's chairman, Representative Darryl Carlyle from Massachusetts. Carlyle, an undergraduate classmate of Tallis's at Harvard, had previously consulted Tallis in 2008 because of his expertise concerning the history of US civil–military relations. Early during the first term of the new Democratic administration, Carlyle was engaged in setting up the US House of Representatives Commission on Wartime Contracting in Iraq and Afghanistan.

During Tallis's testimony on drones two years later, he seemed distraught. He chose, at the last minute, simply to read verbatim from the testimony of a previous witness, the legal scholar Mary Ellen O'Connell. Her work focuses on international law and the use of force. Tallis then proceeded to go beyond his allotted time to read quickly and disjointedly some paragraphs from a paper he had published some years before on President Eisenhower's January 1961 "military-industrial complex" speech. Tallis clumsily made a rushed argument that what that speech cast as a warning about a looming future danger was in fact a cloaked confession. He said he had found a document that proved that outgoing President Eisenhower was in fact announcing, in a veiled way, that he had failed to prevent Pentagon generals' usurpation of control over US military and foreign policy through their retention of all important decision-making over US nuclear weapons and war planning.

The last words of Tallis's testimony were from a memo he had discovered in a folder holding several early drafts of Eisenhower's speech. The memo came originally from the archives of the Truman administration and was written by a staff member at the Pentagon. Tallis read aloud the military aide's comment that "from that moment in August 1946 on, there was a general agreement at the highest levels of government that henceforth the civilian branches would continue to pretend to give orders and we in the Pentagon would pretend to obey."

After his testimony at the end of April 2010, Tallis gradually descended into a state of near total silence. In 2015, his doctors diagnosed his condition as a rare form of "severe adult selective mutism with occasional apparent symptoms of malignant catatonia." As I write this introduction to selections from his notebooks, Tallis has resumed his silence after some months recently of having exhibited increased verbal and affective responsiveness both during visits from myself and his daughter, Cary Martinson-Winslow, and in interactions with staff.

I believe that Tallis's present emotional and psychological state can be traced back to what he experienced on the morning of April 28, 2010. For the entire twenty-minute duration of his sworn testimony before the committee, I believe he was experiencing the intense shock of the absolute loss of faith in the power of the words by which he had hitherto lived. I believe he suddenly experienced the loss of the sense that he could trust the world he had previously confidently known and helped to shape as a responsible beneficiary and highly regarded narrator and interpreter of American power. Until the moment of his testimony he had believed in what he considered to be the fundamental good faith of the underlying democratic narrative of his nation's continuity. At that Congressional committee hearing his faith in that narrative suddenly became impossible to sustain. His participation in its logic, he wrote later in an entry, suddenly felt criminal.

From the moment of his testimony before the committee, I believe Tallis retreated into the composition of his notebook entries as a place of refuge—a temporary respite from personal terror and panic. He had been keeping notebook entries almost daily since he experienced a quasi-vision in Sheep Meadow in Central Park in November of

2003. After what he experienced as his "failed testimony," he tried to use his notebooks as a means of creating, "at whatever cost," "an entirely new method for practicing historical justice."

Every entry in the notebooks bears a notation Tallis calls its "template marking." In the original notebooks many entries bear more than one. A few entries bear as many as six. My best surmise is that the first template marking almost always identifies the place within the cycle of Tallis's meditative practice of his evolving "method of historical justice" that generated the composition of that particular entry. Subsequent template markings designate, I believe, meditative returns by Tallis to that entry and his decisions about where his associations while rereading it led him to place his immediate contemplation within his overall system of "creating durations of a just reciprocity."

In this presentation of selections from the notebooks I have elected for the most part to use only one of the template markings for each entry, always the first unless otherwise indicated. In a few instances I have been governed by my best understanding, through my own practice of my brother's method, of an entry's indispensable contribution to a full understanding of my brother's vision. In these few cases, I have listed an entry's multiple template markings and have left it to the reader to decipher the implications for that entry's overall importance to Tallis's method as he himself practiced it.

Tallis's method, he wrote in an entry late in 2010, was the only way he could conceive of "getting from one moment to another in a bearable way." "From now on," he wrote, he was determined to make his method his "exclusive means of combining intervals of duration with ethically coherent continuities of expression." He wrote that his notebooks were his "laboratory for my urgent experiment." "New durations of historical justice," he said, "are what I find myself most wishing for myself and others as citizens of our country and beneficiaries of empire."

I suggested to Tallis's doctors that what he considered his culpable failure to influence policy through his testimony before the Congressional committee triggered the onset of the acute phase of his illness. They did not, as I expected, summarily dismiss my theory of his present condition's origin.

As I have said, in early December of 2015, Tallis voluntarily committed himself to the Lakehill Long-Term Psychiatric Care Facility in upstate New York near Lawrence College, where he taught for over twenty-five years. By then he had stopped speaking almost entirely and displayed increasing signs of disorientation and dissociated thinking. The doctors said their diagnosis was highly unusual but not inconsistent with behaviors sometimes exhibited by patients of Tallis's high intelligence and intellectual background. The doctors emphasized that they based their cautiously optimistic (despite the severity of Tallis's symptoms) prognosis regarding partial or perhaps even full recovery partly on the extremely labile but ideationally rich content of his interior thought revealed in the notebook entries I showed them. Tallis has resided at the Lakehill facility for almost three years now.

I write this introduction to a selection of entries from Tallis Martinson's notebooks as his longtime editor and younger brother—"by eight minutes." We are identical twins. I am now also his legal guardian and the literary executor of his estate. Tallis's one request of me was a promise that I would never permit electroconvulsive therapy (ECT)—electroshock—to be used no matter how severe the symptoms of his illness might continue to be. I gave him my word I would not. It was a promise I could not keep.

I have devoted myself over the past two and a half years to learning to practice Tallis's historical method. My hope is that eventually this will help me reach him despite the persistence of his prolonged silence during my most recent visits. I want to find a way to get closer to him. I find myself wanting something entirely new to happen between us. I sometimes find myself imagining a sudden change occurring in both of us simultaneously, perhaps during a walk on one of the forest paths winding through the facility's extensive wooded grounds. Or maybe the change will come as we wordlessly sit facing each other in the large dayroom on Lakehill's first floor. I hope such a moment comes soon.

Thankfully Tallis's mutism is no longer accompanied by the acute and prolonged episodes of anxiety and muscular agitation he experienced during his first weeks of hospitalization. The doctors continue to be optimistic that the mutism will eventually lift. They continue to remind me that with continued good health, he could regain his powers of intellect and ordinary personal communication at any moment.

For the past three years, Tallis's daughter—my niece, Cary—and I have visited him at least twice every month for a day. Sometimes we stay for two. We often make the trip together. Each of us also visits him separately as our schedules permit. Both of us live in New York City, so we are able to adhere to this regular visiting schedule without too much difficulty. Until very lately, Tallis's condition has shown signs of moderate improvement. Until his recent and, we hope, temporary setback, he had come to recognize us immediately on sight in the visitors' dayroom and even seemed at times to welcome our company. I am happy to report that he no longer stares vacantly and indifferently around the room, avoiding our gaze. He sometimes smiles, and recently each of us, at different times, has had the feeling that, just for an instant, he wanted to engage us. Then with a frown and vigorous flailing of his arms, he seems each time to reject the impulse. We and the doctors are nevertheless cautiously optimistic that Tallis's mental deterioration has been arrested and that recovery is not impossible. Cary and I are careful to counsel each other not to expect too much too soon.

In the spring of 2016, I was prompted by Tallis's publishers to go through my brother's papers. The head of the imprint that published the three-volume edition of Tallis's *History of U.S. Civil–Military Relations, 1783–1975* wanted to know if somewhere there wasn't perhaps a working draft of a fourth and final volume. Had Tallis not perhaps brought his major historical project up closer to the present? Given the present turmoil of contemporary political events and military confrontations, Tallis's publisher said, he and his colleagues were eager to publish a new edition of his history with the addition of a new fourth volume covering the years 1975 to 2015. He said he had discussed this idea with Tallis from time to time beginning soon after the American invasion of Iraq in March of 2003.

I could not find any completed or partial drafts of such a work. (I did find a few preparatory notes giving tentative titles of possible additional chapters for an updated version of the original work.) In the course of my search, however, I decided to read more carefully than I had previously the 126 notebooks along with Tallis's instructions regarding them. I read them to see if they shed light on why Tallis had not continued work on a final volume of his history with his usual discipline and thoroughness.

In his instructions, Tallis said the notebook entries constituted what, as early as 2005, he found himself referring to privately as his "Daybook from Sheep Meadow." As best I can now make out, the entries were composed, almost without skipping a day, between November 3, 2003, and April 5, 2015. I take him at his word when he writes, "These entries provide a rough record of my thoughts and mental condition as I developed and practiced my historical method for refusing empire after the vision I experienced in Sheep Meadow at approximately 2:00 PM the afternoon of November 3, 2003."

I recommended to Tallis's publisher that he commission another historian to write a fourth volume for Tallis's history of American civil–military relations. I mentioned that I would be transcribing, selecting, and annotating entries from Tallis's notebooks for possible publication as an entirely separate work. Tallis's publisher said he would be pleased to consider any manuscript I produced along these lines. He emphasized that the house could not commit to anything before they had been able to look at a rough completed draft of such a work.

What follows are excerpts from a much longer draft manuscript of my edited and sometimes extensively annotated entries from Tallis's notebooks. For this compilation, I have chosen entries, mostly from the later years, roughly from the time of his Congressional testimony in the spring of 2010 to his last entry, written in April of 2015. For some entries I have felt obliged to provide extensive explanatory material. This is because the entries often contain cryptic references to a family and personal history that I am able to fill in for the obvious reason that Tallis and I grew up in the same house and shared the same childhood. Without such annotation readers will not be able to follow the logic of many of the associations Tallis makes in his entries or to identify the immediate biographical and personal sources of their emotional intensity.

Several times in the notebooks Tallis speaks of "my ecstasy of ordinary perception just before I saw the missiles strike." For a long time, I did not know how to interpret this statement or what weight to give it in Tallis's own practice of his method. I now believe it is his shorthand for the dislocation and destruction of agency in which he felt implicated through the US government's illegal use of unmanned drones to assassinate official enemies and other members of hostile populations beyond an active battlefield. He uses the phrase, I think, as a placeholder to designate his own experience of the distracted, discontinuous, even pleasurable apprehension of war's lived temporality that, as he says in another entry, "creates a rending, flaying ecstasy of complicity in the exterminatory history we are now living together as beneficiaries."

For all its despair, one virtue of Tallis's experiment, I believe, is that his method proposes a habitation of the duration of American history different from any we have had before. It is a duration that cannot be measured by any narrative of peace and war we have conventionally recognized. That habitation, I believe his entries are intended to prove, entails an ecstatic reciprocity made from common speech we are all aware we know but which we have never dared to speak with the fluency that would make it our own. In the end, Tallis believed he had failed in his experiment. The pain of his silence now fills reciprocity's evacuated space. I want to prove him wrong.

FROM THE NOTEBOOKS OF TALLIS MARTINSON
November 27, 2003

—This swirl of objects, this haze of thought—the light these days cannot contain: this beginning. [I.1; II.1; III.1a–1b; IV.1; V.1]

Template explanation (shorter version):

I.1; The first of seven epigraphs: *As soon as thought dries up, it is replaced by words. We begin to exchange set phrases, not noticing that all living meaning has gone from them. Poor, trembling creatures—we don't know what meaning is. It will return only if and when we come to our senses and remember that we are responsible for everything.* (Nadezhda Mandelstam)

II.1; The first of five chapters: "Sworn Testimony Is Direct Evidence" (Part of a judge's charge to a jury in every civil and criminal trial)

III.1a–1b; The first of three sets of interpretive antinomies: 1a. We are social all the way down; 1b. By far the greatest use of language is for thought and not communication, despite virtual dogma to the contrary. (Noam Chomsky)

IV.1; The first of a trajectory of three founding literary texts of Western civilization: *Miserere mei, Deus,*

secundum magnam misericordiam tuam. (Psalm 51
Unto the end. A Psalm of David when the prophet
Nathan came to him after he went into Bathsheba:
"Have mercy upon me, O God, according to thy
loving kindness")

V.1; The immediacy of Anagoge (three scenes from
Sheep Meadow): 1. St. Michael in Trees; 2. St.
Anthony's Gaze; 3. The Painted Word. (From two
paintings by Hieronymus Bosch: *The Temptation of St.
Anthony* and *St. John on Patmos.*) The texts of the template should be memorized verbatim and the paintings
stored in memory for the fluency of my method to
produce its full effect. [A full outline of Tallis's historical method is provided beginning on p. 131.]

Authorization for the meditative application of this
template to texts and thoughts requiring our interpretation is
provided by eschatology understood as knowledge concerning last things—death, judgment, heaven, hell, the end of
history, and the end of a sustainable natural world. A French
prisoner of war who spent three years in a German intern-
ment camp during World War II wrote after his release:

The eschatological notion of judgment implies that
beings have an identity before eternity, before the
accomplishment of history, before the fullness of
time, while there is still time. The idea of being overflowing history makes possible beings called upon

to answer at their trial and consequently beings that can speak rather than lend their lips to an anonymous utterance of history. Peace is produced as this aptitude for speech. The eschatological vision breaks with the totality of wars and empires in which one does not speak. It does not envisage the end of history within being understood as a totality but institutes a relation with the infinity of being which exceeds the totality. The first 'vision' of eschatology (hereby distinguished from the revealed opinions of positive religion) reveals the very possibility of eschatology, that is, the breach of the totality, the possibility of a *signification without a context*. The certitude of peace is not to be obtained by a play of antitheses. The peace of empires issued from war rests on war. It does not restore to alienated beings their lost identity. For that a primordial and original relation with being is needed.   (Emmanuel Levinas)

From the Notebooks of Tallis Martinson
July 10, 2013

—My artificial ecstasy of vision in Sheep Meadow on Monday, November 3, 2003: Let yourself see this: the unarmed black helicopter, with no markings, hovers deafeningly above the field in which all the couples stand beside their small children and embrace each other—some standing, some prone—in the sudden summer warmth of November's surprising sun. The temperature that afternoon reached a record high of seventy-nine degrees Fahrenheit by 1:00 PM. The poet sings from the side of the hill beneath a terraced tree while the helicopter's loud rotors create a maddening, illiterate wind. Everyone suddenly understands that the loud noise provides cover for the sound of the copilot's voice inside the helicopter's cockpit calling the drone strike in. [I.6; II.2; III.3a–3b; IV.3; V.3]

I.6; Epigraph 6: *Daughter, from far away he visits you / whom you have come to love / out of the river of yourself, / not the Yalu or the Mississippi. / Here his different eye / (presence is the knowledge that when you renew the world, / all worlds will be renewed)—/ a stone, white water.*

II.2; Chapter 2: "John James Audubon, Aged Six, in Couëron, France, in the Midst of Revolution, Dreams of Looking Up in Saint-Domingue in 1791"

III.3a–3b; Argument by antinomy (third of three sets): 3a. Our present history of permanent wars is being narrated to us as a military emergency in which the principle of order is itself at stake. Under these conditions the violence of power becomes its own self-justifying, self-legitimizing argument from which there is no appeal in political or moral speech. 3b. Fundamental historical change occurs when poets turn themselves into instruments for the metamorphosis—the withholding and unfolding—of *literary* time that the rest of us have ceased to hear but which gets narrated to us nevertheless as the source of determining cultural structures. Between the act of listening and the act of speech delivery there is another activity that come closest to being performance and constitutes its essence, so to speak. The unfilled interval between listening and speech delivery is silent, absurd to its very core. We cannot obtain meaning by asking others the truth of our passage across that interval in language generated by thought. (Osip Mandelstam)

IV.3; A trajectory of the founding texts of Western civilization (third of three): You must not blame yourself. The simple truth is this: during my first deployment I was made to participate in things the enormity of which is hard to describe. War crimes, crimes against humanity. Though I did not participate willingly, and made what I thought was my best effort to stop these events, there are some things that a person simply cannot come back from. I take some pride in that, actually, as to move on in life after being part of such a thing would be the mark of a sociopath in my mind. These things go far beyond what most are even aware of. (From the last letter of Daniel Somers, dated June 10, 2013)

V.3; The immediacy of Anagoge (three scenes from Sheep Meadow, third scene, The Painted Word (after Hieronymus Bosch's *St. John on Patmos*)): The radiance of joy in the Virgin's glance as she effortlessly dictates the words for the imminence of the Apocalypse through an angel with a peacock's wings to the handsome, smiling youth, Saint and Scribe, holding the upraised quill on Patmos. The tiny merchant ship entering the harbor far below is on fire. Nothing that will ever happen can possibly disrupt or detract from the unbounded happiness of this scene.

•

EDITOR'S NOTE (**Christopher Renthro Martinson [CRM]**)

At the risk of pedantry, I will now proceed to use this entry of July 10, 2013, to present, in a more complete form, as clearly and succinctly as I can, using Tallis's own words wherever possible, the rules he devised for practicing his "entirely new method of enacting historical justice." Here is how he explained his procedures for composing his notebook entries in a long letter to me dated January 12, 2015:

"I eventually learned to compose each entry after performing a preliminary mental exercise visualizing our father, Justin Martinson, in the early fall of 1943, just outside Naples, reading the first three cantos of Dante's *Inferno* for the first time in Italian. Our father is reading from a battered, once expensive, leather-bound volume he had found lying unscathed in a pile of books scattered across the floor of a room without a ceiling. Looking up, Father's gaze is open to the sky from inside the ruins of a villa American planes had bombed earlier in the week. This happened near the town of Avellino sometime around September 28, 1943. Father had been drafted at the age of twenty-five from Yale graduate school, where he was an advanced Ph.D. candidate in classics. The army sent him to Officer Candidate School. His knowledge of German and linguistics made him valuable as a cryptographer. After officer training, he was assigned to the Signals Intelligence Corps.

His discovery, he said, in the midst of war, that because of his previously acquired knowledge of Latin, Greek, German, French, Hebrew, and Sanskrit, he could speak and read Italian without having studied it felt to him like a miracle. The *Inferno*, he said, was the first poem he had ever made his own without any effort whatsoever. When I was fourteen (the year was 1964), Father spoke to me with an urgency and intensity that seemed to assert (with an authority beyond argument) that I would understand what he was about to say. He told me it was 'as valuable as life itself to learn Italian by sound if only to be able to take inside the body through one's own voice and mind *verbatim* all 414 of the first three cantos' lines.' 'After you do that,' he said, 'translation will forever register on your ears and mind as irrelevant—translation will always be for you a contradiction in terms.'

After our father's death and after my vision in Sheep

Meadow, at the age of fifty-four, I finally memorized the first three cantos of *Inferno* for myself. After months of effort, I began to decipher without a translation the syntax and the sound assembled crudely from my faulty knowledge of Latin, French, Spanish, and a little German and Greek. I refused to put pressure on myself concerning what this obsessive, doubling activity of mine might mean. After my failed testimony before the House committee in 2010, I newly understood the necessity of our father's and now my discipline to create, in the midst of the self-canceling hypocrisies of complicity, rules for a principled refusal of a militarily imposed continuity."

•

EDITOR'S NOTE (CRM)

After successfully beginning my compilation of selections from my brother's notebooks, I suddenly became stuck for a whole year. I could not proceed. The entries kept coming back to Tallis's meditations on the moment our father, Justin, read Dante for the first time as a young American soldier near Naples in a room without a ceiling in a bombed-out villa. I could not understand why. I sensed it was somehow where Tallis understood our father came to himself in language without constraint—without the burden of failed or betrayed interpretations. After a year of not knowing why I was stuck, I decided to give up on the entire project. It was at this moment that I suddenly experienced the intense memory of the following scene. It was a memory I could not remember having brought to consciousness in over thirty years. All at once I felt flooded with an understanding of why reading Dante in the bombed-out room without a ceiling meant so much to Tallis. It meant so much to him because of what I thought I now understood it had meant to our father—and yet now I think I know that neither Tallis nor our father, Justin, ever let themselves acknowledge its real import or its true source.

The event that left the memory I am referring to occurred in either 1955 or 1956, I'm not sure which. I am five or six years old and looking up into the wild, terrified, abject cruelty and violence of unresponsiveness—an annihilating coldness—of the eyes of our grandfather, Tallis Martinson Sr. His gaze is his incomprehensibly unreciprocating answer to my own spontaneous look's attempt to express the unprotected depth of my love for him. My joy in him is that he is the father of my father, Justin Martinson, his firstborn son. Therefore, I am his. I am trying with my look to honor him as my father's and my own invaluable, indispensable, unbounded source. Grandfather was born in 1891. Grandfather Tallis and I are alone and standing in summer afternoon light on the banks of a pond in upstate New York. He is supposed to be taking me fishing, but I can see now he only wants to return to the house to be by himself at his desk cutting out scenes of animals from hunting magazines. He is desperate and enraged and suffocating. My look has interfered with his failing internal efforts to suppress his constant, terrified rage. I am over-whelmed with the knowledge that something in me has failed him.

Even now in memory I find myself desperately trying to love him and failing. I remember myself as a child real-izing that this was a new kind of knowledge. I remember knowing even then that it could not be used. If I did not love him, I knew I hated him. The surprise of it made me wonder what knowledge was for.

There was no protection for my crime. In my reaction to my grandfather's gaze I now realize I directly felt what our father had once felt toward the same man—before and after language. As an infant he had waited with his mother in a huge house in Elizabeth, New Jersey, endlessly desiring (through her) his soldier father home from World War I. Trying to love my grandfather and failing, I suddenly thought I knew what our father, Justin, had never let him-self know as an adult. No father had ever returned to him, aged eighteen months in June of 1919, in this man's disas-trous homecoming from the battlefields of France.

Looking at my grandfather that afternoon in 1955 or 1956, I knew suddenly that there was only brokenness. I felt my own fury that he was using the adult violence of his authority to force me to go through the motions of pre-tending that he stood there whole as the completed man who we (I, Tallis, my sister, my mother, Grandmother, and above all, my father) needed him to be. I felt his refusal to reciprocate the neediness of my loving gaze silently condemning me without appeal for a primordial betrayal that I was not entitled to survive.

This sudden memory gave me access to another memory from later that same year. Sometime in October, a few miles from that same pond, I am standing in the back seat of my grandparents' Buick sedan holding on to the back of the front seat as we traveled along a dirt road through second-growth forest. Again, it was in late-afternoon light. My grandmother was driving. Her lips were quivering. I had first noticed this newly acquired habit a few days previously. Suddenly, Grandfather, who was sitting beside her in the front seat, ordered her—impatiently, angrily—to stop the car. His voice sounded both excited and panicked. As he reached beside him on the seat, I saw for the first time the stock of the breached double-barreled shotgun resting there, barrels pointing at the car floor. The next thing I knew I was standing beside him outside the car, looking up to his face as he silently aimed the gun at the sky. A loud, dry clatter of wings had just risen from the underbrush beside the road. After the second explosion I saw an object falling from the sky. It fell straight down with a terrifyingly swift finality of unwinged, weighted catastrophe. Moments before I had felt the rush of Maggie, my grandfather's retriever, bumping me in her frenzied leap through the car's open back door.

With what I experienced then, and still think now, was love, Maggie leaped to retrieve the fallen bird and carry it back to Grandfather in her soft mouth. Maggie's trembling body seemed to express an ecstasy of purest joy. In one breath, Grandfather cursed her and himself—himself for missing his first shot, her for leaving before he had given her the permission of his command. My grandmother did not get out of the car. The trip home was filled with a tense, desolate silence that radiated a violence I had never before encountered.

With the remembering of this scene came the realization that I had never spoken of this event to anyone. I realize now, as I try to reconstruct the occasion's details, that Tallis must have been with me. I hope to ask him about this when he recovers. I will not be at all surprised if he says he remembers that afternoon perfectly. If so, I will ask him why we have never once spoken of it to each other in all these intervening years.

Tallis Martinson Sr. was not present at the birth of our father, Justin, who was born on December 19, 1917. This was because our grandfather was among the first American soldiers to arrive in France in June of 1917. He had volunteered to fight as an enlisted man. He sent home word that he wanted to have a holster with a loaded pistol hanging from one of the bedposts during his first son's birth. His wish was complied with. Tallis Sr. had volunteered to serve as a member of the Fifth Field Regiment and was assigned in October to fight alongside the French in the trenches around Nancy. He participated in the American victory at Cantigny on May 28, 2018. He was part of the artillery support for the American offensive at Belleau Wood between June 6 and June 26, 1918, in which 10,000 US troops were killed, wounded, or missing in action. He returned from World War I in June of 1919.

Emma Wright, our father's favorite cousin (Father himself never spoke to Tallis or me about any of this), told me when I asked about my grandfather that as a child she overheard uncles and aunts saying that Grandfather Tallis returned from WWI utterly changed. He had shed, they reported, the spontaneity and exuberant playfulness for which he had been known. His infectious optimism, his faith in things, was gone.. Clearly, something had happened to him in the war that left him embittered, moody, quick to rage, watchful. He seemed both aggressive and fearful. He appeared both frightened of being overwhelmed and angry that he could not overcome his fear. Emma recalled family members' shock at barely being able to recognize him. Our father, Justin, never spoke of any such traumatic transformation in his father's life. I don't think he could let himself recognize it. His childhood was filled with the arrival of brothers and sisters—six—all but one of whom lived into adulthood.

What came to me when I remembered this scene was the sudden knowledge (a knowledge I do not think Tallis shares) of the significance of his emphasis in his entries of our father as a young soldier reading Dante in Italian, a language Justin did not know before 1943. The fact is that this story of our father reading Dante in a broken room open to the sky near Naples was the *only* story our father ever told us of his wartime experiences. He spent more than two years fighting in Europe during World War Two. (He landed in North Africa in the spring of 1943 and ended up in Vienna in 1945.)

I think I now know that our father had to find a way, in order to help or even rescue *his* father, of *not* knowing that his father never returned home as a coherent self to his wife and infant son from World War I. Denial of this truth created a devouring hole at the center of everything. For Justin to be loyal to his impaired father and still return whole himself (how could he survive *his* world war if his father had been unable to?), our father had had to experience himself anew in a language that gave him his sudden ecstatic doctrine of "no translation." Does war destroy the coherence of everyone who experiences it close up—both living and dead? Is it the refusal of this knowledge (whose family history Tallis's notebook entries document) that Tallis himself was trying to break through?

Our father devoted his scholarly career to writing a book analyzing the aesthetic and moral unity of Homer's *Odyssey*. I asked him when I was young why he did not prefer the *Iliad*. He said then he had no answer to that. I now think it was because the *Odyssey* is about a warrior king's successful return from war to wife and son after twenty years. I think our father used it all his life as an unacknowledged, uninterpreted counterhistory with which to pretend that his soldier father returned to him whole from France in 1919.

In support of my theory, I feel compelled to add that

in Canto 26 of the *Inferno*, Dante tells the story of Ulysses quite differently from the way Homer does. In Dante's account, Ulysses refuses father, wife, son, and home and, for the sake of knowledge, sails not to Ithaka but west through the Gates of Hercules to the end of the world. There by the divine malice of a sudden storm he is plunged, unrealized and unfulfilled, with all his men, to the bottom of the sea from within sight of the gate to redemption and the path to paradise. In a poem whose meanings our father swore resisted all translation (whose meanings were identical to their words' sounded duration in the immediacy of air) he found a way to experience the contradictory truth of a narrative whose true generative logic he never found a way to permit himself to know.

It is not my purpose in making Tallis's notebooks public to expose family secrets. Nevertheless, I feel compelled to add to this account of our grandfather and our father's relationship to him another family matter that concerns me personally. I include it here because it strongly affected all my relations to the history that animates my brother's notebooks and my present annotation of them.

Along with the notebooks in one of the boxes Tallis left in my custody, I found six bundles of family letters tied with string. The number totals more than 175, and they cover a period of more than forty years. (In his accompanying note, Tallis appoints me the letters' owner and literary executor and gives me control over access and all publication rights.)

The earliest letter is addressed to Tallis from Sari Moreland, the daughter of a close friend and colleague of our father at the college, Roger Moreland, a professor of English. The envelope bears a postmark of late May of 1970. Sari was born the same year as Tallis and I. I have stayed in touch with her at long intervals over all these years.

Since the content of the letters will prove relevant to how Tallis's notebook entries will be interpreted and how his method will be used by readers, certain personal family matters do need to be divulged here at the beginning. I had fallen in love with Sari at first sight at the age of five and boldly announced to Tallis that whether or not he loved her too, I would never love anyone again the way I loved her. Nothing, I immediately told him (at the age of five), would ever stop me from marrying her. I knew beyond doubt that we would be joined forever just the way protagonists are married at the end of fairy tales. In fact, when we were six, at Sari's instigation, we performed a wedding ceremony for ourselves beside a trash can of burning wastepaper in the backyard of my parents' house. We had been assisting my father with that weekly chore. He had just gone back inside the house after asking us to keep an eye on the fire for him. When we were eighteen, Sari rejected me as a boyfriend. She preferred by then the company of other, more rebellious, more dangerous men. "You feel too much like a brother," she said.

Even as I write these sentences, I can still feel the pulse

and spell of the evening light (I cannot remember now if it was spring or fall) of our first childhood meeting. We stood facing each other in the front hall of her parents' home. She stood against the curving banister leading upstairs, the animated grace of her child's form framed against the backdrop of the white banister's spindles that seemed about to be set ablaze by the splintering light. She seemed to appear from the pages of an illustrated children's book. Its unknown story was my happiness. I knew from that moment I could trust my desire. The world needed no revision. Sometimes practicing my brother's method I have felt that moment continuing into the present.

I cannot remember for certain if Tallis was with me during this moment. I assume that he was. I vaguely remember worrying that he might feel exactly what I was feeling. Then I remember thinking there was nothing I could do about that—that nothing could stop me from loving her and the consequences were what being was for. I am preparing myself to ask Tallis when he feels better if he recalls this moment that I have kept so carefully in mind all this time.

Tallis's letter to me explaining the rules of his method contains a reference to his memorizing the cantos from the *Inferno* as instructed by our father:

"Each morning after recalling from memory in the original language, as Father taught us, one of the first three cantos (I have not progressed beyond these three), I allow myself the luxury of free, associational speech derived from the applicable generative template I have pre-assigned to that day's meditation."

In my own efforts to interpret Tallis's notebook entries I have found it useful to keep in mind this practice of reciting the *Inferno* cantos in the original Italian as a preliminary exercise to recording his spontaneous thoughts. It was his way perhaps of trying to join our father in his refuge from his estrangement from his father (Tallis Sr.'s) unacknowledged brokenness, his—to a child—untranslatable failure to return as an intact soul from France in 1919. Tallis doesn't mention Dante further in his template directions but goes on to say the following:

"I created the template for spontaneous association gradually in the course of the four months following my vision in Sheep Meadow in November of 2003. I have altered the template slightly from time to time to keep it up to date. These variations are minor and do not need to be dwelt upon here. (The one major revision of the template is the substitution, after June 22, 2013, of the last letter of Daniel Somers in place of Osip Mandelstam's fragment from "Ode to Stalin" as the fifth epigraph in the first section of the template and as the third text in the trajectory of founding texts in Western civilization in the template's fourth section.)

"My rules were admittedly patchwork but also a successful solution to the immediate crisis of my need for another continuity of American history to assert moment to moment. I now realize this procedure need not be as desperate as I so often make it out to be. Though arduous, I do not hesitate to recommend that you commit each element of my template to memory. This will take time, but I dare to hope you will find the benefits worth the effort.

"I hasten to add that you are by no means confined in your meditations to the template I have devised. My method will prove its usefulness if it leads you to devise a different one with another set of rules of your own invention that you are able to hold constantly in memory and employ effectively. The task is always the same: to narrate without complicity your own success in refusing the permanence of American wars."

•

EDITOR'S NOTE (CRM)

Here again is the second of the notebook entries typed on the folded piece of frayed typing paper I found lying loosely in one of the cardboard boxes holding the notebooks. The entry is dated November 7, 2004. The transcription of it below bears a different template designation from the one given it on the loose piece of typing paper [I.2; II.1; III.2a–2b; IV.2; V.2]. The transcription below bears the template designation that appears in the original of this entry recorded in the notebooks [I.1; II.2; III.3a.–3b; IV.1; V.2]. The event in the Iraq War corresponding with this date was the beginning of the Second Battle of Fallujah, which lasted until December 23, 2004. In time you will get used to bringing to mind from memory verbatim the same note-book entry while using the different template notations assigned to it to generate variant associations. "The contrasting patterns of association this mnemonic procedure generates," Tallis writes later in a note to me, "will help you to use my new method for accomplishing historical justice effectively to traverse the interval between one moment to the next without unwarranted constraint or fear."

FROM THE NOTEBOOKS OF TALLIS MARTINSON
November 7, 2004

—This sweetness in the bone—a new kind of light—this failure of democracy and the success of empire—a lust past all possession fulfilled in delight—a violence no one wanted to survive—an ecstasy of unanswerable force, a place of ease past every betrayed possibility of reciprocity. In Sheep Meadow that afternoon a year ago, I felt my thought and ordinary American ecstatic perception become one. [I.1; II.2; III.3a.–3b; IV.1; V.2]

> I.1; Epigraph 1: *As soon as thought dries up, it is replaced by words. A word is too easily transformed from a meaningful sign into a mere signal, and a group of words into an empty formula, bereft even of the sense such things have in magic. We begin to exchange set phrases, not noticing that all living meaning has gone from them. Poor, trembling creatures—we don't know what meaning*

is; it has vanished from the world. It will return only if and when people come to their senses and recall that we must answer for everything. (Nadezhda Mandelstam]

II.2; Chapter 2: "On August 21, 1791, at the Age of Six, John James Audubon Dreams of Looking Up in Saint-Domingue in Couëron, France, near Nantes"; Audubon, his biographer tells us, was born a bastard in 1785 on his father's Les Cayes sugar plantation in Saint-Domingue (soon, in 1804, to become Haiti). His mother was a French chambermaid who died just months after his birth. He was raised on the island until he was six with his younger half sister, Rose, daughter of his father's "quadroon" mistress, Catherine "Sanitte" Bouffard. Of these lives we know almost nothing. His illegitimate birth and early deep association with slavery were closely held secrets all Audubon's life. There seems to have been trauma, one biographer suggests, mastered by a manic, obsessive love for wild birds. The slave uprisings on nearby islands and the beginnings of revolution in France and Saint-Domingue led his father to sell the plantation shortly before the Haitian Revolution began on August 21, 1791. His father sent for him and his sister from Nantes in June of that year. There is no record, this same biographer says, of what happened "to whoever mothered him on Saint-Domingue."

III.3a–3b; Argument by antinomy: 3a. Contemporary history is narrated to us as a state of military emergency in which the exercise of the violence of state power constitutes the self-evidence of its legitimacy. The violence of power has become its own justifying argument asserted in the immediacy of real time. 3b. Historical change occurs when poets turn themselves into instruments of the metamorphosis—the withholding and unfolding—of the *literary* time that the rest of us have ceased to hear but which nevertheless gets narrated to us as the source of "cultural structures." (Osip Mandelstam)

IV.1; A trajectory of founding texts of Western civilization: Psalm 51 (*Miserere mei*) The Psalm of David when the prophet Nathan came to him after he went into Bathsheba:

"Behold, thou desirest truth in the inward parts:
    and in the hidden part thou shalt make me to
    know wisdom.
Purge me with hyssop, and I shall be clean: wash
    me, and I shall be whiter than snow.
Make me to hear joy and gladness; that the
    bones which thou hast broken may rejoice.

V.2; The immediacy of Anagoge: 2. St. Anthony's Gaze: "Now since you asked me to give you an account of the blessed Antony's way of life, and are wishful to learn how he began the discipline, who and what manner of man he was previous to this, how he closed his life, and whether the things told of him are true, that you also may bring yourselves to imitate him, I very readily accepted your behest, for to me also the bare recollection of Antony is a great accession of help. And I know that you, when you have heard, apart from your admiration of the man, will be wishful to emulate his determination; seeing that for monks the life of Antony is a sufficient pattern of discipline." (Athanasius, Patriarch of Alexandria)

FROM THE NOTEBOOKS OF TALLIS MARTINSON
November 7, 2004
(continued later in the afternoon):

—This painting instead—Hieronymus Bosch's triptych of Anthony's temptations, the ecstasies of them: the naked woman in the hollow tree draped in crimson cloth, all her beauty forfeit; all the cities are burning; all the writings are snares; the sudden immediacy of God's presence in the human heart (this subjectivity was made possible some say by the influence of the desert fathers on popular consciousness after subjection to Roman occupation and rule)—this immediacy of God's unlettered presence has become the new text to be deciphered. Before Anthony's example the church fathers' authority had been derived from mastery of philosophical writings (Christian and

Pagan) preserved on the expensive pages of rich men's codices.

•

EDITOR'S NOTE (CRM)

This same notebook entry must be read differently when it bears different template markings. The November 7, 2004, entry typed on the loose sheet of paper Tallis left for me to find in the fall of 2015 must be read not against the association with Audubon's birds and childhood on a sugar plantation in Haiti, but against the associations with Tallis's testimony on the morning of April 28, 2010. In the autograph of the notebook in which this entry appears, Tallis inserted three typed pages containing the transcription of the testimony of a witness who had spoken to the committee before him, Kenneth Anderson, a legal and policy expert on national security law. His testimony reads:

Legal Adviser to the State Department, Harold Koh, in his recent speech on March 25, 2010, said four things concerning the legality of the use of armed drones by US personnel: 1) that the targeting of individual persons beyond an active battlefield was not illegal because it was US military practice to do so during World War II; 2) that the sophistication of new technologies had no bearing on the ethics of the use of weapons with the possible exception if it increased the indiscriminateness of casualties (the opposite he found to be the case with drones); 3) that the use of drones against targeted individuals without legal process or due warning did not constitute the war crime of extrajudicial execution because in fighting terror the United States has the right to defend itself with lethal force in an international context separate from armed conflict as a technical legal and constitutional matter; and 4) that there has long been a ban on domestic political assassination but that "assassination" has never been legally or legislatively defined.

Beneath this transcription of testimony Tallis has typed the following long note: "Elsewhere Anderson said he had been heartened in his testimony before the committee by the opinion of a former Legal Adviser to the State Department who in a lecture at a law school in 1989 had said that 'targeted killings in self-defense of the state as the object of terrorism have been authoritatively determined by the federal government to fall outside the assassination prohibition.' But no such international legal justification of self-defense exists in the wording of Article 51 of the UN Charter, which speaks only of the right of self-defense against 'an armed attack against a member of the United Nations.' The preemptive right of self-defense, established by the *Caroline* case, requires that there must exist 'a necessity of self-defense, instant, overwhelming, leaving no choice of means, and no moment of deliberation,' and furthermore that any action taken must be proportional, 'since the act justified by the necessity of self-defense, must be limited by that necessity, and kept clearly within it.' No conceivable meaning of threat to the American nation posed by terrorists meets these criteria for justifying the lawless, agentless impunity of the anonymous murder of unidentified individuals beyond the battlefield now being systematically perpetrated by persons acting in the name of the United States through the use of drones."

Immediately following the transcript of Professor Anderson's testimony, Tallis has typed more testimony from another witness at the hearing, Professor Mary Ellen O'Connell, an expert on the law of just wars. This was the testimony he read verbatim at the hearing instead of reading from his own prepared text. Aloud, he told them: "Drones are not legal for use outside active combat zones . . . Restricting drones to the battlefield is the single most important rule governing their use. Yet, the United States is failing to follow it more often than not. The United States Congress has not declared war. We would have it that we are a peaceful nation pursuing foreign enemies who have attacked us. At the very time we are trying to win hearts and minds to respect the rule of law, we ourselves are failing to follow its most basic rule. . . . But the battlefield is a real place. Battlefields and armed conflicts are not fictions created by lawyers. . . . Outside of a war or an armed conflict, everyone is a civilian when it comes to the use of lethal force. Armed conflicts cannot be created on paper, in a legal memo that then translates into the right to kill as if you were on a real battlefield. . . . Only a lawful combatant may carry out the use of killing with combat drones. The CIA and civilian contractors have no right to do so. . . . We know from empirical data, and this is my final point, that the use of major military force in counterterrorism operations has been counterproductive. A Just War doctrine teaches that we should always and only use force when we can accomplish more good than harm."

•

EDITOR'S NOTE (CRM)

Early on in my editing of his notebooks, I joined Tallis and our father, Justin, in learning by heart the first three cantos of Dante's *Inferno* in the original Italian—a language I too never formally learned and have never spoken out loud. (All of us, perhaps, are trying to bring our fathers home inside a language whose sound of immediacy and ground of truth are unrelated to translation.) In memorization I sometimes sense the mind being given access to language's spontaneous and unbounded generation of the next word within another duration of continuity. I sometimes feel the memorized phrases fighting assimilation by an algorithm in the present generating a violence of determination whose logic of thought as monetization overrides the lines' original oral duration of potential reciprocity. I took it upon myself to add the following exercise of verbatim memorization to juxtapose against our father's doctrine of "no translation": "The concept of *algorithm* is used to define the notion of *decidability*. That notion is central for explaining how *formal systems* come into being starting from a small set of axioms and rules. In *logic* the time an algorithm requires to complete cannot be measured, as it is not apparently related to our customary physical dimension. From such uncertainties that characterize ongoing work, stems the unavailability of a definition of *algorithm* that suits both concrete (in some sense) and abstract usage of the term."

•

FROM THE NOTEBOOKS OF TALLIS MARTINSON
November 8, 2004

—How, in our cowardice, are we to inhabit the next word now?

> *Poscia ch' io v'ebbi alcun riconosciuto,*
>   *vidi e conobbi l'ombra di colui*
>   *che fece per viltà il gran rifiuto.*
> *Incontanente intesi e certo fui . . .*
>   [from *Inferno*, Canto 3]

(After I saw and recognized some of them / I saw and knew the shade of him / who through cowardice made the great refusal. I suddenly understood and knew with certainty. . .)

[I.1; II.3; III.3a–3b; IV.3; V.1]

I.1: As soon as thought dries up, it is replaced by words. . . .

II.3: On Burdicks Hill

III.3a. The history we are living is being narrated as a military emergency. 3b. Structural change occurs when poets turn themselves into instruments of the metamorphosis of *literary* time . . .

IV.3: The piles of heads disappear in the distance. / I am diminished there. No one / will remember my name. But in the sound / of the rustle of pages and children's games / I will rise from the dead to say / "the sun." (Osip Mandelstam)

V.1: St. Michael in Trees at the head of his armies . . .

•

EDITOR'S NOTE (CRM)

My personal association to this entry: my vision of Sari on first meeting her as a child. Her worth. This cowardice: my father's, my brother's, and now my own. How are we to remake my father's doctrine into something valuable after all this time?

•

EDITOR'S NOTE (**CRM**)

January 25, 2018

Late in assembling this volume of selections from
Tallis's notebooks, I made the decision to introduce
to my practice of his method a terza rima of rhymed
thoughts instead of Dante's rhyming sounds (in which
our father so strongly believed). I use this rhyme scheme
as my personal accompaniment to the noise of the helicopter's rotors over my brother's head during his vision
in Sheep Meadow. With this additional mental noise I
sense I will be able more accurately to track my brother's descent into silence. Dante's scheme of "chained"
end rhymes for his eleven-syllabled lines can be repre-
sented like this:

a,b,a; b,c,b; c,d,c; d,e,d; etc., *ad infinitum*

My scheme for meditating upon my brother's entries is
made from three sets of rhymed thoughts as a backdrop
against which to interpret his entries' progress toward his
present agitated, sometimes catatonic silence:

a,b,c; c,a,b; b,c,a; a,b,c; c,a,b; b,c,a; a,b,c; etc.

To more accurately reproduce the noise in my mind
against which my reading of my brother's notebooks takes

place, I employ the overlay of the cross-rhythm (using the same sets of thoughts) established by hearing their serial simultaneity, three over four, within the same duration as an entry's contemplation. Like this:

a,b,c; | c,a,b; | b,c,a; | a,b,c; | c,a,b; | b,c,a,|
a,b,c; | c,a,b; | b,c,a; | a,b,c; | etc.

a,b,c,c; | a,b,b,c; | a,a,b,c; | c,a,b,b; | c,a,a,b; |
c,c,a,b; | b,c,a,a; | b,c,c,a; | b,b,c,a; | a,b,c,c; |
etc.

(This exercise takes patience at first. Of course, you must choose thoughts of your own if you find mine to be inadequate to the task of creating in the mind an accurate accompanying sound for a just American history.)

Here are my three sets of a *terza rima* of thought:

1.

a: Donald J. Trump is a mirror not an aberration.

b: We lack a language adequate to the history we are living.

c: This has happened many times before and has often generated new forms of thought and expression.

2.

a: The undecidability of the word.

b: The exterminatory productivity of global capitalism.

c: The intuition of a universal mutual intelligibility and therefore of a potentially universal historical justice implicit in the fact of the natural human language faculty.

3.

a: The frayed scrim of continuity made from clichéd fragments of an American exceptionalist triumphalism. (One of these is: "We the People.")

b: The intuition of an ecstatic history of universal reciprocity as a counternarrative to accounts of New World slavery motivated by its beneficiaries' perceived interests in minimizing the continuing enormities of its harms.

c: A new history of print-culture literacy as the anticipatory creation in the midst of material abundance of a nonmonetized duration of thought for the practice of an unbounded reciprocity among equally valued lives.

Why do we still lack a popular vernacular form for the truth of the news of the exterminatory history we are living with which successfully to refuse it?

Everyone will readily agree that it is of the greatest importance to know whether we are not duped by morality. Does not lucidity, the very openness of the

mind upon the true, consist of catching a glimpse of
the permanent possibility of war?

(Emmanuel Levinas)

Entries from Tallis Martinson's Notebooks:

April 5, 2010

—Lyrically—lightly—does it—St. Michael in Trees;
St. Stephen getting even: The child shot by American soldiers from the helicopter after the journalists were killed:
the left leg severed just below the knee: "This one will
live." This question of knowledge; this question of fact;
this question of act and its disclosure. [I.7; II.3; III.1a–1b;
IV.1; V.1]

April 18, 2010

—Every moment flows evenly toward a white field
filled with commonplace thoughts and the sound of
untranslated—suddenly untranslatable—speech. [I.4; II.2;
III.1a–1b; IV.1; V.1]

August 2, 2010

—Sweet Lord: This hand toward her in the New
World light: This destruction was not planned. I swear this
by what I know. This mechanical revolution—this absence
of help: Now this lust amid the screams of the heathen:
This perfection of Grace lying behind what we did: I will
guard admittance through its door: A lasting joy. A coyote

lopes across a field bordered by stone walls that were made and abandoned years ago—the last time Englishmen pushed this far into the alien land. [I.5; II.2; III.2a–2b; IV.2; V.2]

August 18, 2010

—The November sun, this warmth of wind heard in the upper branches—against nature, as if the birds were speaking their enormous happiness in human tongue—untranslatable by anyone. Then, after we begin to hear it, we realize that it is the sound of helicopters' rotors that we have been waiting for all along—ever since we left Saigon. St. Michael in Trees. [I.6. II.2; III.3a–3b; IV.3; V.3]

August 19, 2010

—The wind when it comes will counsel caution and bring a plague. Your armies are scattered. Bright metal reflecting a child's perfect will and purpose. We caused this, and it happened: there will be no time soon in which to remember—no place from which to know the perfection of its logic as a sweetness of mind. [I.1; II.2; III.2a–2b; IV.1; V.3]   [I.1; II.3; III.2a–2b; IV.2; V.2]

November 4, 2010

—A fall into history—this book of November reveries from gardens of earthly delight: a Puritan drone against the play of interpretations: a master narrative for the sake of lyrical presence—an opening onto absolute power. An event—however inconsequential—has to imply a redemptive logic to be coherent—listening to birds without distraction, listing their sightings with a pencil in a battered notebook; St. Michael in Trees—rumors of his promised victory. [I.2; II.2; III.2a–2b; IV.2; V.1]   [I.2; II.3; III.3a–3b; IV.3; V.3]

January 27, 2012

—Print literacy's fixed point of view enforces the deferment of justice until some narrative end to all of history. Until then, we victors are off the hook—accidental enablers of perfection behind the back of our own actions in collusion with the state—however criminal its official acts formally may be judged to be at the end. By then we will have learned to repent and achieve the reconciliation necessary for final victory. [I.3; II.4; III.1a–1b; IV.1; V.1]

August 16, 2012

—There is goodness too in history. It shouldn't be so hard to find: this ability to create wealth out of flows through the body—and flows of bodies—in time. Why does love give way to the rage to possess beyond the limits of a just reciprocity? In the moment of thought we are each other. Unlimited possession is also a lasting duration we have made no provision to survive.

Our father, Justin, falsely gentle—a fierce child; our father, against translation—believer in the immediacy of the word, bringing his father home in his mind from

France in June of 1919 before a child has access to word-logic, *aetat* eighteen months: all the guns in Europe exploding in both the infant and his father's failing thought. [I.4; II.4; III.2a–2b; IV.2; V.2]

March 2, 2015

—No peace beyond the line. *Donna è gentil nel ciel che si compiange* [There is a blessed lady in heaven who feels such pity] / Haiti just above my head: These painted birds. [I.5; II.4; III.3a–3b; IV.3; V.3]

April 5, 2015 (The Notebooks' last entry)

—Birds at an angle of flight—something is falling there beneath them—inside a place of thought: St. Michael will lead all God's armies of light—by what sign will his certain victory over every evil be made manifest? Oh, to be among his foot soldiers on that day! [I.6; II.5; III.1a–1b; IV.1; V.1]

April 28, 2004	First airing by CBS of report documenting systematic torture by US personnel of Iraqi prisoners at Abu Ghraib
November 7, 2004	The Second Battle of Fallujah begins and lasts until December 23
April 2, 2005	Battle of Abu Ghraib prison

April 5, 2010:	Release of gunsight footage from July 12, 2007, of an air-to-ground attack by two US AH-64 Apache helicopters in Baghdad that killed seven unarmed men, including two journalists, and severely wounded two children
April 18, 2010	Iraqi Special Operations Forces kill ISIL's leadership, Abu Ayyub al-Masri and Abu Omar al-Baghdadi. A US Black Hawk UH-60 helicopter supporting the operation crashes killing a Ranger sergeant and injuring the aircrew
August 2, 2010	*The New York Times* announces partial withdrawal of US troops
August 18, 2010	The official end of US effective combat operations in Iraq
August 19, 2010	Operation Iraqi Freedom officially ends
November 4, 2010	Ayman al-Zawahiri threatens new attacks on the US

January 27, 2012	A suicide bomber in Baghdad kills 33 people and wounds 65 others
August 16, 2012	A series of bombings kills more than 90 people across Iraq
March 2, 2015	Coalition of Iraqi Armed Forces and militia numbering around 30,000 launch an offensive against Islamic State positions in Tikrit

FROM THE NOTEBOOKS OF TALLIS MARTINSON
November 5, 2010

—I have decided, in the midst of my practice of my new method of historical justice, to draft, in the liberal manner, an essay titled "The American Dream as Secular Transcendence." I want to state in the old way (without my template's scaffolding) the truth, to which this essay's way of speaking has contributed, that the enormities of practical transformation (including self-transformation) required for the enactment of the universal equality called for in the Declaration of Independence are of such a scale and such a fundamental nature as to render the idea of their actual achievement either hallucinatory or derisory in the opinion of most beneficiaries of the nation's values and institutions. The essay will go on to argue that in the violence of the incoherence issuing from such fundamental contradictions between vision and reality lies the ground for a new language of reciprocity that bears inside it a new history—and therefore a new experience and valuation—of equality. American neoliberalism's astounding success in global wealth creation through capitalist extraction (the sheer monetized quantity of worth, interpreted cooperatively, proves that dearth has been abolished) has now been revealed to be exterminatory. The sudden immediacy of the apocalyptic crisis of duration, meaning, and value now facing us renders derisory the coerced optimism of gradualist incremental reform. Equality as intersubjectivity no longer has an unlimited unaccomplished future into which it can be projected and postponed. The present universal crisis overflows the thought that thinks it. Are new thoughts and acts within new durations of reciprocity already amongst us? How will we enact the new history such thoughts make possible?

•

EDITOR'S NOTE (CRM)

"The idea of being overflowing history makes possible *existents* [*étants*] both involved in being and personal, called upon to answer at their trial and consequently already adult—but, for that very reason, *existents* that can speak rather than lending their lips to an anonymous utterance of history. Peace is produced as this aptitude for speech. The eschatological vision breaks with the totality of wars and empires in which one does not speak. It does not envisage the end of history within being understood as a totality but institutes a relation with the infinity of being which exceeds the totality." (Emmanuel Levinas).

The overwhelming accumulation of history that gets lived never gets told. But it may always get said in ways that have yet to be accurately interpreted. The right words are never missing. This, I conclude, is the central argument of Tallis's notebooks. But interpretations that would allow the words to inhabit a peaceful coherence lack agreement. The immediacy of historical justice eludes us as a practiced duration of thought.

The afternoon before my mother died in the spring of 1998 at the age of eighty-two, she told me something about Sari that her manner of speaking insisted I needed to know. It was as if she had waited for the last possible moment to tell me. We were alone in the hospice-care room of her nursing home. She had always been aware of my childhood love for Sari. She was high on the morphine that she administered to herself from a pump she controlled to keep at bay the pain of lung cancer, which had spread to her spine. Out of nowhere she started to speak of an incident that had occurred when Sari and I were fourteen. She could still hear, she suddenly said, the sound of Sari's father's voice (Roger Moreland, a professor of literature at the college) boasting during a drunken, intimate, late-night party that he had slept with both his daughters when they were children. He did it, my mother said he explained, to prove the transcendence available to someone who truly practiced the aesthetics of ecstasy. "Everyone," she said he insisted, "had benefited." She said she could remember his words as if he were still speaking them aloud in the room. The sensorium, he claimed, offers ecstasy as a perfected continuity to the cultivated sensibility. His acts, he said, proved that consciousness was intended to move "from peak to peak with no descent into the troughs of ordinariness."

I thought my mother was hallucinating—that what she was articulating was a fragment from an unguarded fantasy created by her mind in its last disintegrating moments. The violence of the desecration of which she spoke so calmly and directly was not interpretable, I decided, even as I was hearing it—by me or by anyone else.

I did not tell anyone what my mother had said for seventeen years. But then in 2015, Sari sent me, after her father and mother had both died, a photograph taken of my mother and her father sitting together on a couch holding drinks. The photograph seemed to have been taken in the early 1970s. The expression on my mother's face immediately made me recall her words the day before she died. Underneath her expression's resigned, tentative, and pleading engagement with the camera, I saw a rage of aversion. Her look seemed to betray a hatred of helpless self-doubting, and a yearning for a speech for a true history she lacked the confidence to imagine as her own. The camera seemed to have captured a silence, made from sitting next to this man that forced her to be absent from herself everywhere.

It was after seeing this photograph, that I spoke to Tallis, seven months before he committed himself to Lakehill Psychiatric Center. I asked him if our mother had ever said anything to him about Sari's father's drunken confession. "No," he said, "but I overheard the adults who had been at the party talking about it for days afterward." (It was then that I realized that the party had happened in June of 1964, early in the summer I was away from home at music camp.) Tallis and I were fourteen.

Tallis has known the truth of the history my mother told me for over fifty years but has never spoken of it to me. This fact transfigures me. No adult who was at that party— including my father, my mother, and Sari's mother—as far as I know, ever did anything to try to help either child. An unsurvivable impunity of respectability held—and continues to hold—sway.

CHAPTER 1

Sworn Testimony Is Direct Evidence

FROM THE NOTEBOOKS OF TALLIS MARTINSON
July 14, 2010

—Henceforth meditations on historical justice will require the frequent recitation from memory of the following formal definition of language: "Language is a combinatorial system capable of generating an unbounded number of creative expressions interpretable at two interfaces: the cognitive/intentional and the sensorimotor (roughly, thought and sound)." The success of the American state in creating democracy depends upon the exercise of the right of revolution undertaken to accomplish the self-evident truths of equality to be enjoyed and practiced through the exercise of the universal equal right to life, liberty, and the pursuit of happiness. Surely historical justice consists in getting from one moment to the next inside the enjoyment of these events narrated according to the principles (and from an embodied point of view) of an ordinary shared duration from which no one is excluded and from which no one is ever found to be missing. The following is what

I said, reading directly from the sworn testimony of Mary Ellen O'Connell, an expert on the legal doctrine of just war, in my own sworn testimony on April 28th before the House committee hearing on the legality of the US use of unmanned armed drones for targeted assassination beyond a battlefield: *Outside of war or an armed conflict, everyone is a civilian when it comes to the use of lethal force. The combatant's privilege to kill on the battlefield without being charged with a crime applies inside an armed conflict and not outside. Armed conflicts cannot be created on paper, in a legal memo that then translates into the right to kill as if you were on a real battlefield.*

[I.3; II.2; III.2a–2b; IV.1; V.1]

I.3; Epigraph 3: *What matters in poetry is only the understanding that brings it about.* (Osip Mandelstam)

II.2; Chapter 2: "On August 21, 1791, at the Age of Six, John James Audubon Dreams of Looking Up in Saint-Domingue in Couëron, France, near Nantes"

III.2a–2b; Argument by antinomy: 2a. Order is derived from public assemblies of armed men; the object of war is to secure the peace; the object of peace is to foresee war and to win it by every means. 2b. Every society tells itself an origin story that contains a narrative of the ending of the world. No one who has ever lived is ever found to be missing from a single one of these stories.

IV.1; A trajectory of founding texts of Western civilization: 1. Psalm 51, King David's confession of guilt: *Tibi soli peccavi, et malum coram te feci; ut ius-tificeris in sermonibus tuis, et vincas cum iudicaris.* (Against thee, and thee only, have I sinned, and done this evil in thy sight: that thou mightest be justified when thou speakest, and be clear when thou judgest.)

V.1; The immediacy of Anagoge: 1. St. Michael at the head of the armies of three religions on the last day. His approach is first evident in the violence of the wind tossing the tops of the trees bordering Sheep Meadow.

•

EDITOR'S PERSONAL NOTE (CRM)

Beneath this entry, Tallis has hand-copied (with errors as if transcribing from memory) the following passage from Theodore Dwight Weld's introduction to his *American Slavery as It Is* (1839):

"'The foregoing declarations . . . are not haphazard assertions, nor the exaggerations of fiction conjured up to carry a point; nor are they the rhapsodies of enthusiasm, nor crude conclusions, jumped at by hasty and imperfect investigation nor the aimless outpourings either of sympathy or poetry; but they are proclamations of deliberate, well weighed convictions, produced by accumulations of proof, by affirmations and affidavits, by written testimonies and statements of a cloud of witnesses who speak what they know and testify what they have seen, and all these impregnably fortified by proofs innumerable, in the relation of the slaveholder to his slave, the nature of arbitrary power, and the nature and history of man. Between the larger divisions of the work, brief personal narratives will be inserted, containing a mass of facts and testimony, both general and specific."

●

EDITOR'S NOTE (CRM)

I write: "Confession: while assembling these entries in July of 2019, I have come to the hardest part. In the midst of a broken going on being, I have been reading my brother's notebooks as if they could save me. Rather than give in to doubt I have been pursuing his peace made from historical justice as an available duration and recruiting others for my comfort and peace of mind. Memorization and its associations have produced durations that feel momentarily valuable—as if there were a duration of completion without regret; a duration that suspended—as if it could be dissolved—this present interval between rage and paralyzing fear.

FROM THE NOTEBOOKS OF TALLIS MARTINSON
July 14, 2010 (*cont.*)
(Hand-copied by Tallis from *American Slavery as It Is* (1839))

—"Narrative of Mr. Caulkins: The scenes that I have witnessed are enough to harrow up the soul; but could the slave be permitted to tell the story of his sufferings, which no white man, not linked with slavery, is allowed to know, the land would vomit out the horrible system, slaveholders and all, if they would not unclinch their grasp upon their defenceless victims. [p. 11]

Testimony of Mr. William Poe:

"In traveling, one day, from Petersburg to Richmond, Virginia, I heard cries of distress at a distance, on the road. I rode up, and found two white men, beating a slave. One of them had hold of a rope, which was passed under the bottom of a fence; the other end was fastened around the neck of the slave, who was thrown flat on the ground, on his face, with his back bared. The other was beating him furiously with a large hickory." [p.26]

From the transcript of a drone attack in Afghanistan in the early morning hours of February 20, 2010, obtained through a Freedom of Information Act (FOIA) request:

"DRONE PILOT: Can you zoom in a little bit, man, let
'em take a look?

SENSOR OPERATOR: At least four in the back of the
pickup."

From the introduction to *The Divine Ascent* by John Climacus,
written about 650 CE, a work the renowned scholar Peter
Brown argues "marks the end of late antiquity":

"The miraculous virtues of detachment: Who in
the outside world has worked wonders, raised the
dead, expelled demons? No one. Such deeds are
done by monks. It is their reward. People in secular life cannot do these things for, if they could,
what then would be the point of ascetic practice
and the solitary life?"

*In war reality rends the words and images that dis-
simulate it, to obtrude in its nudity and in its harsh-
ness. Harsh reality (this sounds like a pleonasm!), harsh
object-lesson, at the very moment of its fulguration
when the drapings of illusion burn, war is produced
as the pure experience of pure being. The ontological
event that takes form in this black light is a casting into
movement of beings hitherto anchored in their identity,
a mobilization of absolutes, by an objective order from
which there is no escape. The trial by force is the test of
the real.*   (Emmanuel Levinas)

From the Notebooks of Tallis Martinson
October 11, 2010

—Waiting for the arrival of St. Michael: lightly, lightly does it. This is the way it was always going to end. With this violence. With this grace. Don't say the .30-caliber bullets the gunships use are alien. There is video of the event. This mechanical wind—its noise. Your pleasure—your commitment to the scene—contributes verisimilitude. Was this a battle? Was this the boy reading—dreaming himself—into a heroic murder scene? The sun's warmth is contagious and full of lust. [I.4; II.4; III.1a–1b; IV.1; V.3]

•

EDITOR'S NOTE (CRM)

I hope the reader will have begun to be able to read the template notation without assistance. I will continue to provide shorthand reminders of Tallis's memorized texts, whose full versions can be found starting on page 131.

I.4; Epigraph 4: 709 Hard Year. Sir Gottfried died. (Annals of St. Gall)

II.4; Chapter 4: "The Invasion of Cambodia on Crane's Beach, May 1, 1970"

III.1; Argument by antinomy: 1a. We are social all the way down; 1b. By far the greatest use of language is for thought and not communication, despite virtual dogma to the contrary. (Noam Chomsky)

IV.1; A trajectory of texts: Psalm 51

"Behold, thou desirest truth in the inward parts:
and in the hidden part thou shalt make me to know
  wisdom.
Purge me with hyssop, and I shall be clean: wash me,
  and I shall be whiter than snow.
Make me to hear joy and gladness; that the bones
  which thou hast broken may rejoice."

V.3; The Immediacy of Anogoge (three scenes from Sheep Meadow): 3. *St. John on Patmos* or The Painted Word

CHAPTER 2

On August 21, 1791, at the Age of Six, John James Audubon Dreams of Looking up in Saint-Domingue in Couëron, France, near Nantes

FROM THE NOTEBOOKS OF TALLIS MARTINSON
August 6, 2010

—A tangled darkness has taken over the light in the former openness of the neighbor's fields. His abandoned farm expects no future—no moment of remembrance. Brightly colored birds fly and sing. Doesn't every child who has loved a parent attempt to do this: inhabit a "hermetic enchantment as a young hero within the timeless"—"establish a *nunc stans* (to use a formula of the scholastics) to embody the word's aim to be that which it speaks, forgetting the condition of life as a condition of narration—throwing overboard all the god-conditioned forms of human knowledge"? (Thomas Mann) [I.3; II.2; III.3a–3b; IV.3; V.2]

I.3; Epigraph 3: What matters in poetry is only the understanding that brings it about. *Imagine something intelligible, grasped, wrested from obscurity, in a language voluntarily and willingly forgotten immediately after the act of intellection and realization is completed. Poetry is not a part of nature, not even its best or choicest part, let alone a reflection of it—this would make a mockery of the axioms of identity; rather, poetry establishes itself with astonishing independence in a new extra-spatial field of action, not so much narrating as acting out in nature by means of its arsenal of devices, commonly known as tropes.*   (Osip Mandelstam)

II.2; Chapter 2: "On August 21, 1791, at the Age of Six, John James Audubon Dreams of Looking Up in Saint-Domingue in Couëron, France, near Nantes." Bankrupt in 1819, Audubon sells two slaves in New Orleans. He has traveled with them for two weeks in a skiff down the Ohio and Mississippi Rivers from Henderson, Kentucky. He must procure money to repay his debts. One of the slaves he sells may have been the servant who saved his life when he fell into quicksand while shooting birds. Audubon never wrote a word about any of these events. We know them now only indirectly from public records.

III.3a–3b; Argument by antinomy: 3a. Our present is narrated to us as a state of emergency in which order itself is at risk. The exercise of the unlimited violence of state power has become the self-evidence of its legitimacy. The appeal to the argument of "self-defense" to justify impunity (as in the use beyond the battlefield by the most powerful state in the world of unmanned lethal weapons of war against targeted individuals with attendant collateral civilian damage) is a non sequitur. 3b. Fundamental cultural change occurs when poets turn themselves into instruments for the metamorphosis of *literary* time—the withholding and unfolding of the literary time the rest of us have ceased to hear but which nevertheless gets incessantly cited to us as the basis of so-called "cultural structures."

(Osip Mandelstam)

IV.3; A trajectory of founding texts of Western civilization: 3. "The piles of heads disappear in the distance;/ I am diminished there. / No one remembers my name,/ but in the rustle of pages and the sound of children's games,/ I shall return to say:/ "the sun!" (Fragment from Osip Mandelstam's "Ode to Stalin")

IV.2; The immediacy of Anagoge (three scenes from Sheep Meadow): 2. St. Anthony's gaze: You can't describe it: Sari's beauty. In the painting depicting the saint's temptations, these signs of evil and of many pleasures; these demons under the tree—this violence, this fragmentation—this brokenness in all its common uninterpretable signification. Reading and writing won't save you—not then, not now. Just letters on a page like the other rendered details—God's word. The saint looks up from the book he holds to return your gaze. The only scripture to be deciphered now—in this moment (the kindness in his eyes implies)—is the human heart. "He could not endure to learn letters, not caring to associate with other boys. All his desire was, as it is written of Jacob, to live a plain man at home." (Athanasius) After his own battles with demons alone in his cell, Anthony was able to cure hallucinations and the pains of ergotism: St. Anthony's fire. All his happiness.

•

EDITOR'S NOTE (CRM)

I have not yet recorded my own response to this entry using my brother's method. I have, however, applied to it the following *terza rima* of thought not sound, arranged in the usual pattern (three over four):

a: The undecidability of the word.

b: The exterminatory productivity of global capitalism.

c: The intuition of a universal mutual intelligibility and therefore of a potentially universal historical justice implicit in the fact of the natural human language faculty.

a,b,c; | c,a,b; | b,c,a; | a,b,c; | c,a,b; | b,c,a; |
a,b,c; | c,a,b; | b,c,a; | a,b,c; | c,a,b;

a,b,c,c; | a,b,b,c; | a,a,b,c; | c,a,b,b; | c,a,a,b; |
c,c,a,b; | b,c,a,a; | b,c,c,a; | b,b,c,a; | a,b,c,c; |
a,b,b,c;

FROM THE NOTEBOOKS OF TALLIS MARTINSON
August 6, 2010 (cont.)

[Copied in Tallis's handwriting from *American Slavery as It Is: Testimony of a Thousand Witnesses*, edited by Theodore Dwight Weld (1839)]:

—"The sufferings are not only innumerable, they are *indescribable*. . . . I *cannot describe* the daily, hourly, ceaseless torture, endured by the heart that is constantly trampled under the foot of despotic power. It mocks all power of language. Who can describe the anguish of that mind which feels itself impaled upon the iron of arbitrary power—its living, writhing, helpless victim! every human susceptibility tortured, its sympathies torn, and stung, and bleeding—always feeling the death-weapon in its heart, and yet not so deep as to *kill* that humanity which is made the curse of its existence." [Angelina Grimké, p.57]

"There can be therefore no offence against the state

for a mere beating of a slave, unaccompanied by any circumstances of cruelty, or an attempt to kill and murder. The peace of the state is not thereby broken; for a slave is not generally regarded as legally capable of being within the peace of the state. He is not a citizen and is not in that character entitled to her protection." [*American Slavery as It Is*, p.146]

01:05

SENSOR OPERATOR: That truck would make a beautiful target. OK, that's a Chevy Suburban.
PILOT: Yeah.
SENSOR OPERATOR: Yeah.

01:07

MISSION INTELLIGENCE COORDINATOR: Screener said at least one child near SUV.

I spent eleven winters, between the years 1824 and 1835, in the state of North Carolina, mostly in the vicinity of Wilmington; and four out of the eleven on the estate of Mr. John Swan, five or six miles from that place. There were on his plantation about seventy slaves, male and female.

The fourth step of spiritual ascent is obedience: "The robber was astounded by the voice of the superior coming from the sanctuary. (He swore afterwards that he thought he heard thunder and not a human voice.)

At once he fell on his face and he trembled and shook with fear. While he lay on the ground, moistening the floor with his tears, the marvelous healer turned to him, trying everything so as to save him and to give everyone else an example of salvation and true humility. Before all, he exhorted him to describe in detail everything he had done. Terrified, the robber confessed all, sins of the flesh, natural and unnatural, with humans and with beasts; poisonings, murders, and many other deeds too awful to hear or to set down on paper. Everyone was horrified. But when he had finished his confession, the superior allowed him to be given the habit at once and to be included in the ranks of the brethren." (John Climacus)

> *But does not the experience of war refute escha-*
> *tology, as it refutes morality? Have we not begun by*
> *acknowledging the irrefutable evidence of totality?*
>
> *To tell the truth, ever since eschatology has*
> *opposed peace to war the evidence of war has been*
> *maintained in an essentially hypocritical civilization,*
> *that is, attached both to the True and to the Good,*
> *henceforth antagonistic. It is perhaps time to see in*
> *hypocrisy not only a base contingent defect of man,*
> *but the underlying rending of a world attached to both*
> *the philosophers and the prophets.*
>
> (Emmanuel Levinas)

FROM THE NOTEBOOKS OF TALLIS MARTINSON
September 30, 2015

—A beginning of sense: a running forward and backward as if he were in a battle. A disciplined narrative of the possible rhythms of permanence has gone missing. A disciple of finance said that it could be defined as "time and the right to choose to have value." How is this statement of value to be made into democracy? Unless historical justice is now funded—explicitly tied to making the past and the present whole in specified relation to absolute loss, there can be no way to distinguish democracy from a managed consent to the status quo. (Robert Meister)

Christopher told me yesterday afternoon that the day before she died, in May of 1998, our mother told him that Roger Moreland announced drunkenly at a party in the late spring of 1964 that he had slept with his daughters, with both Sari and her sister, when they were children, as young as nine or ten. Christopher had not believed her. He thought she was hallucinating. It was true that she was under the influence of the morphine she administered to herself freely from a pump to relieve the pain from the cancer raging in her spine. There had been other instances during those last days when she spoke and laughed as if addressing and responding to persons in the room present only to her. I had to tell him that I knew that the events of the party and Sari's father's confession were true—that, at the age of fourteen, I had overheard the adults who had been there talking animatedly about it several times in the course of a few days. Christopher was away at music camp. I always let myself believe somehow that Christopher knew what had happened that evening. I couldn't be the one to tell him.

What did our mother not want lost with her death by telling Christopher this history at the very end? The truth that we belonged to a class whose responsibility for our acts lacked adequate language, adequate speech? That impunity was a legacy neither she nor we had any business believing we could honorably survive? That the truth of her complicity—in the crime of refusing to help or address the harm done to two children—needed to be said out loud as a way to open the way for registering the infinite value of all lives.

CHAPTER 3

On Burdick's Hill

FROM THE NOTEBOOKS OF TALLIS MARTINSON
October 30, 2010

—This light, this wealth, this entitled ecstasy—too intense to value. . . . The wind, when it comes, will counsel caution and bring a plague. Your armies are scattered. Bright metal reflecting a child's perfect will. We caused this to happen. Soon there will be no time in which to remember it—no place from which to know the perfection of its logic as a sweetness of mind. [I.1; II.3; III.2a–2b; IV.1; V.3]

> I.1; Epigraph 1: As soon as thought dries up it is replaced by words. A word is too easily transformed from a meaningful sign into a mere signal, and a group of words into an empty formula, bereft even of the sense such things have in magic. We begin to exchange set phrases, not noticing that all living meaning has gone from them. (Nadezhda Mandelstam)
>
> II.3; Chapter 3: "On Burdick's Hill"

•

EDITOR'S NOTE (CRM)

In the 2015 letter to me that Tallis left inside one of the boxes holding his notebooks he said that after his testimony before the committee in late April of 2010 he took it upon himself to invite those he "deemed it essential to confront" to meet with him in person on Burdick's Hill in Central Park, overlooking Sheep Meadow. There is a bench there, beloved by bird watchers, that he liked, in good weather, to occupy from early morning to mid or even late afternoon when he was free. During the first months of the sabbatical leave he took after he testified in Washington, Tallis stayed with me in New York and visited Burdick's Hill almost every day. In the letter he said he made appointments through the fall of 2010 with seven people, including Cary and me, to meet with him there individually over the course of several weeks but that none of us had ever showed up at the agreed upon time. The people he said he had summoned were Daryl Carlyle, the Democratic chairman from Rhode Island of the House subcommittee hearing on drones (whom Tallis had known in college and who had invited him to testify); Roger Moreland; Sari Moreland; Sari's boyfriend, Gilliam Kell; Cora Mason; Cary; and me. Now that I have learned to practice his method myself, I believe that by the fall of 2015 Tallis had confused his invention and meditative practice of his method with actual conversations with significant others. I remember the sometimes lost, affectless drone of his voice during that period in 2010 when he stayed with me. It was then I also began to notice his increasingly prolonged intervals of agitated silence. It was as if his internal experience of his self's continuity were losing touch with some way to trust a general common ground of mutual engagement. In the autograph manuscript version of the notebook entry for October 30, 2010, the following words after the template marking of [I.1; II.3; III.2a–2b; IV.1; V.3] have been crossed out: "This method, this moment, this combinatorial event instead of memory."

III.2a–2b; Argument by antinomy: 2a. Order is derived from public assemblies of armed men. The purpose of war is to secure the peace; the purpose of peace is to prepare for war and to win it by every means. 2b. Every culture has an origin story that contains within it a narration of the final destruction of the world. No human being who has ever lived is ever found to be missing from any of these stories.

IV.1; A trajectory of founding literary texts of Western civilization: 1. *In finem. Psalmus David, cum venit ad eum Nathan propheta, quando intravit ad Bethsabee. Miserere mei, Deus, secundum magnam misericordiam tuam; et secundum multitudinem miserationum tuarum, dele iniquitatem meam. Amplius lava me ab iniquitate mea et a peccato meo munda me.*

[Unto the end. A Psalm of David when the prophet Nathan came to him after he sinned with Bathsheba: Have mercy upon me, O God, according to thy lovingkindness: according unto the multitude of thy tender mercies blot out my transgressions. Wash me thoroughly from mine iniquity, and cleanse me from my sin.]. . . *Tibi soli peccavi et malum coram te feci ut iustificeris in sermonibus tuis et vincas cum iudicaris.* [Against thee and thee only have I sinned and done this evil in thy sight; that thou might be justified when thou speakest and clear when thou judgest.]

V.3; The immediacy of Anagoge: 3. The Painted Word (the smiling, joyful recorder of Apocalypse's happiness on Patmos, taking dictation directly from the angel standing upon a hillock): Far below, the tiny merchant ship is seen entering the harbor. It is on fire. This ship, its crew we do not see, the scudding white-capped waves, the associations that enable all meaning to be made visible—each moment now belongs to the immediate joy of all things. The artist's patrons have paid handsomely to own this work and have placed it in the private chapel built from the new wealth that flows to them from the New World:

These bright birds of argument—this sugared wealth of absolute possession—this commons of achieved abundance in which we refuse to choose democracy over empire.

•

EDITOR'S NOTE (CRM)

As I assemble these selections I find myself increasingly adept at practicing Tallis's method. I find my thoughts are more fluent than before. I have suddenly remembered myself on the bank of the pond in upstate New York at the age of five trying to love my grandfather and failing. I now sometimes even think I can see the war in France that still holds him, still keeps him from returning to his wife and infant son. What makes every action's accountability to a universal peace of reciprocity seem impossible? When I was eighteen, Father told me that his father, Tallis Sr, once told him, out of the blue, that "what women have to bear is unforgiveable." Because I have now read about the brothels in the villages and towns that were part of the battlefields of World War I, my association goes there. One for officers (marked with a blue lantern), one for the enlisted men (marked with a red one): the long lines of waiting men. How do we imagine a duration of completion that we will not regret? I now feel myself able to get from one moment to the next more easily across the distance of a father-soldier's—two generations gone—constant rage and paralyzing fear. What transcendence—what woman's presence—did our father feel reading Dante without translation near Naples in the fall of 1944? Why do women stay with these broken men?

My *terza rima* of thought not sound (three over four) guiding my practice:

a,b,c; | c,a,b; | b,c,a; | a,b,c; etc.
a,b,c,c; | a,b,b,c; | a,a,b,c; | c,a,b,b; etc.

The second set again:
   a: The undecidability of the word.
   b: The exterminatory productivity of neoliberal
      global capitalism.
   c: The intuition of a universal mutual intelligibility,
      convertible into democratic justice, intrinsic to the
      natural human language faculty.

FROM THE NOTEBOOKS OF TALLIS MARTINSON
October 30, 2010 (cont.)

—Transcribed from memory: "The writer acknowl edges that the book is a very inadequate representation of slavery; and it is so, necessarily, for this reason—that slavery, in some of its workings, is too dreadful for the purposes of art. A work which should represent it strictly as it is would be a work which could not be read; and all works which ever mean to give pleasure must draw a veil somewhere, or they cannot succeed." (Harriet Beecher Stowe, *The Key to Uncle Tom's Cabin* (1854))

From *American Slavery as It Is: Testimony from a Thousand Witnesses*: "READER, you are empanelled as a juror to try a plain case and bring in an honest verdict. The question at issue is one both of law and fact—'What is the actual condition of the United States?'

"One of Mr. Turner's cousins, was employed as overseer on a large plantation in Mississippi. On a certain morning he called the slaves together, to give some orders. While doing it, a slave came running out of his cabin, having a knife in his hand and eating his breakfast. The overseer seeing him coming with the knife, was somewhat alarmed, and instantly raised his gun and shot him dead. He said afterwards, that he believed the slave was perfectly innocent of any evil intentions, he came out hastily to hear the orders whilst eating. *No* notice was taken of the killing.

"Mr. T. related the whipping habits of one of his uncles in Virginia. He was a wealthy man, had a splendid house and grounds. A tree in his *front yard,* was used as a *whipping post.* When a slave was to be punished, he would frequently invite some of his friends, have a table, cards and wine set out under the shade; he would then flog his slave a little while, and then play cards and drink with his friends, occasionally taunting the slave, giving him the privilege of confessing such and such things, at his leisure, after a while flog him again, thus keeping it up for hours or half the day, and sometimes all day. This was his *habit*."

01:07

> MISSION INTELLIGENCE COORDINATOR: Screener said at least one child near SUV.
>
> SENSOR OPERATOR: BULL [expletive] . . . where?
>
> SENSOR OPERATOR: Send me a [expletive] still, I don't think they have kids out at this hour, I know they're shady but come on.
>
> . . .
>
> SENSOR OPERATOR: Well, maybe a teenager but I haven't seen anything that looked that short, granted they're all grouped up here, but . . .
>
> MISSION INTELLIGENCE COORDINATOR: They're reviewing . . .
>
> PILOT: Yeah, review that [expletive] . . . why didn't he say possible child, why are they so quick to call [expletive] kid but not to call a [expletive] rifle?
>
> MISSION INTELLIGENCE COORDINATOR: Two children were at the rear of the SUV.

•

EDITOR'S NOTE (CRM)

I think our father, Justin, always dreamed that reading might become for everyone what it had been for him once in Italy: the end of all translation. I think he always wanted to find that moment again but lost the ability to understand the source of his own desire for such a state of consciousness. Why did he never do anything to try to help Sari—to protect her from her father, his friend and colleague? In what sense, precisely, was there "nothing anyone could do under the circumstances"? Was not my father leaving her all alone to face the same childhood violence in which his own father had failed to return to him in 1919? And why for all those years could I not discern that something had happened that endangered Sari beyond bearing? On her deathbed in 1998 my mother gave me an unnarratable duration requiring the truth of historical justice.

"Look," Father once said to me when I was sixteen, explaining the meaning of *Inferno*'s Canto 2 excitedly, "look at what Dante is saying: the moment has come for everyone to be themselves inside vernacular speech before its truth is controlled by others." Universal thought resides in immediate desire's attention. There is no distraction of interpretation except as aftermath. Vernacular speech is more noble—more deserving of being held in memory—than literary Latin, Dante said, because it is the only language we never have to be taught and constitutes the heart's thoughtful fluency shared by children, women, and men. If only father himself had used it to bring his own father home by recognizing what had happeneed to him. My own thought now, in 2018, reading my brother's words, is "If only someone had used their art to help a child by completing by ordinary act the movement of:

e venni a te così com'ella volse;
d'innanzi a quella fiera ti levai
che del bel monte il corto andar ti tolse.

[And so I came to you as she desired me to; / and freed you from that creature / that stole from you the short way to the beautiful mountain.]

FROM THE NOTEBOOKS OF TALLIS MARTINSON
October 30, 2010 (cont.)

—A popular harrowing—I will read this phrase out loud again before too long. Imagine historical justice as something immediately possible.

In his *Divine Ascent*, John Climacus says, concerning obedience (the fourth step of his spiritual manual's ladder): "A monastery is heaven on earth, so let us tune our hearts like angels serving the Lord. It happens occasionally that those living in this heaven possess hearts of stone. Yet by means of compunction they acquire consolation so that they escape from conceit, and they lighten their labors with their tears. . . . I have often seen such things as these, as Job says (cf. Job 13:1), that is, souls burdened sometimes by slowness of character and sometimes by excessive eagerness. I was astounded by the variety of evil."

*Morality will oppose politics in history and will have
gone beyond the functions of prudence or the canons
of the beautiful to proclaim itself unconditional and
universal when the eschatology of messianic peace will
have come to superpose itself upon the ontology of war.*

FROM THE NOTEBOOKS OF TALLIS MARTINSON
November 1, 2010

—We caused this to happen—this history. The sound
of fire inside the walls of the house. The play of our lethal
contradictions. The autonomy that the language faculty
implies cannot be repealed: this sweetness in the mind due
to the construction of a duration made from the mutual
reciprocity of equals. When representations of historical justice cease to be hallucinatory, peace will occupy the
silence of intervals like the smell of rain. [I.5; II.4; III.3a–3b;
IV.3; V.2]

> I.5; Epigraph 5: "The piles of heads disappear in
> the distance. I am diminished there. . . ." (Osip
> Mandelstam)
>
> II.4; Chapter 4: "The Invasion of Cambodia on Crane's
> Beach, May 1, 1970"
>
> III.3a–3b; Argument by antinomy: 3a. The history we
> are living is narrated to us as a military emergency in
> which order itself is at stake. In such circumstances

the unlimited violence of power becomes its own self-justifying argument. 3b. Fundamental change occurs when poets turn themselves into instruments of the metamorphosis—the withholding and unfolding—of the *literary* time the rest of us have ceased to hear.

IV.3; A trajectory of the founding texts of Western civilization: The piles of heads disappear in the distance. / I am diminished there. No one / will remember my name. / But in the rustle of pages / and the sound of children's games / I shall rise from the dead to say: / "the sun."

V.2; The Immediacy of Anagoge: 2. St. Anthony's Gaze.

CHAPTER 4

The Invasion of Cambodia on Crane's Beach, May 1, 1970

FROM THE NOTEBOOKS OF TALLIS MARTINSON
November 4, 2010

—A fall into history—this book of November reveries from gardens of earthly delight: a Puritan drone against the play of interpretations: a master narrative for lyrical presence—a hypocritical opening onto power's unanswerable impunity. An event—however inconsequential—implies a redemptive logic by virtue of its coherence: listening to birds without distraction, listing their sightings with a pencil in a battered notebook. The wind blows raw and cold against the unprotected skin of wrists and face: St. Michael in Trees—rumors of his promised victory. [I.2; II.4; III.2a–2b; IV.2; V.1]

> I.2; Epigraph 2: By far the greatest use of language is for thought and not communication, despite virtual dogma to the contrary. (Noam Chomsky)
>
> II.4; Chapter 4: "The Invasion of Cambodia on Crane's Beach, May 1, 1970"

III.2a–2b; Argument by antinomy: 2a. Order derives from public assemblies of armed men. The purpose of war is to secure the peace; the purpose of peace is to prepare for war and to win it by every means. The trial by force is the test of the real. 2b. Every society's founding myths include one that narrates the end of the world. No one is ever found to be missing from a single one of these stories.

IV.2; A trajectory of civilization's founding texts: Shakespeare's "Sonnet 77": The vacant leaves thy mind's imprint will bear; / And of this book, this learning mayst thou taste. . . . / These offices, so oft as thou wilt look / Shall profit thee and much enrich thy book.

V.1; The immediacy of Anagoge: 1. St. Michael in Trees: the sudden violence of wind in the tops of trees; the rush of meaning in the bending branches next to Sheep Meadow: "Holiness is presented not so much as a pattern to be imitated, but as a power to be harnessed, and a source of intercession to be supplicated." [Eamon Duffy, introduction to Jacobus de Voragine, *The Golden Legend*]

•

EDITOR'S NOTE (CRM)

From the recent practice of my brother's method (April 13, 2018):

There will be revenge instead of justice for the civil war we didn't have—the one we have postponed until now. We have destroyed countries and populations in the service of a triumphalism whose logic of impunity no practice of democracy has ever interrupted. We were so young then. The fires in the city's streets later that night of May 1, 1970 bore no interpretation we dared to recognize as the nation's end. But fire sometimes stands in for history's accomplishment of embodied universal redemption; such a thought, I think, was in the air. The idea of a self splayed open unrelated to any sign, to any narrative continuity beyond the presence of force constituting its own self-justifying duration. What entitlement is there to ecstasy? Sari's beauty against the backdrop of the gray and white sea: "You may as well be hung for a sheep as a lamb," my mother used to tell me. The necessity of reciting the "neck verse": Under Medieval canon law a death sentence could be commuted to lifetime servitude under ecclesiastical authority if the convicted person invoked "benefit of clergy" by reciting from memory Psalm 51 in Latin: *Miserere mei, Deus, secundum magnam misericordiam tuam.* [Have mercy upon me, O God, according to thy loving kindness.] Professional criminals were said to learn the sounds of the Latin words by heart without any understanding of their meaning in order to reproduce them before a judge at their sentencing. We were all together briefly that afternoon on May 1, 1970, on Crane's Beach in Ipswich, Massachusetts: Tallis; Sari; Sari's father, Roger Moreland (he came later in the afternoon);

Cora Mason; Sari's boyfriend, Gilliam; and me. I cannot remember anything that we said. The sea and the Scotch pines growing on the rocky ledges were beautiful. I remember thinking that the two women's unanswerable beauty overflowed all thought. [I.5; II.4; III.3a–3b; IV.3; V.2]

I.5; Epigraph 5: "I am sorry that it has come to this."

II.4; Chapter 4: "The Invasion of Cambodia on Crane's Beach, May 1, 1970"

III. 3a–3b; Argument by antinomy: 3a. The history we are living is narrated to us as a military emergency in which the principle of order is itself at stake. 3b. Fundamental change occurs when poets turn themselves into instruments in the metamorphosis—the withholding and unfolding—of the *literary* time the rest of us have ceased to hear.

IV. 3; A trajectory of founding texts of Western civilization: 3. "I know how to kill, and I know how to do it so that there is no pain whatsoever."

V.2; The immediacy of Anagoge: 2. St. Anthony's Gaze

•

EDITOR'S NOTE (CRM)

The second element of the meditative template Tallis supplies for each of his notebook entries (designated by the Roman numeral II) refers, he says in his letter of "meditative instructions," "to titles of chapters, as if from a long narrative." Chapter 4, used in my entry above, is titled "The Invasion of Cambodia on Crane's Beach, May 1, 1970." Beginning the afternoon of Monday, November 6, 2003, Tallis seems to have started to plot these storylines as a backdrop for what was to become his "disciplined silence." The five chapters were filled in and were established in their roughly final "form" by the late fall of 2010 or early 2011. By then the chapter titles had stabilized as: 1. "Sworn Testimony Is Direct Evidence"; 2. "On August 21, 1791, at the Age of Six, John James Audubon Dreams of Looking Up in Saint-Domingue in Couëron, France, near Nantes"; 3. "On Burdicks's Hill"; 4. "The Invasion of Cambodia on Crane's Beach, May, 1, 1970"; 5."The Immediacy of Anagoge; Three Scenes from Sheep Meadow: 1.St. Michael in Trees; 2. St. Anthony's Gaze; 3. *St. John on Patmos* or, The Painted Word."

In his 2015 letter appointing me his literary executor, Tallis informed me that in the fall of 2010 he became convinced that it was his duty as an American citizen to summon all of us who had been together on Crane's Beach in Ipswich, Massachusetts, on Friday, May 1, 1970, to meet with him individually on Burdick's Hill. That May Day in 1970 was the day after President Nixon had announced to the nation that United States and South Vietnamese armed forces had invaded Cambodia. The five of us who spent a stunned morning and afternoon in that beautiful place were Tallis, me, Sari, Cora Mason, and Sari's then boyfriend,

Gilliam Kell. Sari's father, Roger Moreland, joined us late in the afternoon. When we returned to Cambridge that evening, we joined rioters in the streets. Storefront windows were being broken and trash cans were burning. Tallis wrote in his 2015 letter that after 2010 he devoted his notebook compositions to preparing himself to question each of us closely about how we narrated to ourselves the continuity we had lived since that day on Crane's Beach. In the late spring of 2013, he said, he even came to believe that he had issued to each of us an urgent invitation to speak with him alone, "face to face," on Burdick's Hill. He thought for a while that our silence meant that we had refused to answer his call. But he came to realize, he said, that in reality he had never contacted us because he himself was at an absolute loss how to answer his own question "within any possible context of good faith." After my own practice of his method, I take my brother at his simplest word: there is an American imperative to make the failure of narrative whose coherence is empire valuable for thought.

From my recent practice of my brother's method:

My *terza rima* of thought, not sound, in patterns of three over four (third set):

a: This patched scrim made from fragments of American nationalist triumphalism.

b: The intuition of a euphoric counterhistory to the history of American slavery in the service of a universal justice waiting to be lived.

c: A new history of print literacy based on verbatim memorization of texts and the reciprocity to be derived from the universal natural language faculty. "Learning to read," he said to his wife concerning me, "would forever unfit him to be a slave." "It was a new and special revelation, explaining dark and mysterious things. . . . I now understood what had been to me a most perplexing difficulty—to wit, the white man's power to enslave the black man. It was a grand achievement, and I prized it highly. From that moment, I understood the pathway from slavery to freedom." (Frederick Douglass)

a,b,c | c,a,b; | b,c,a; | a,b,c; | etc.
a,b,c,c; | a,b,b,c; | a,a,b,c; | c,a,b,b; | etc.

FROM THE NOTEBOOKS OF TALLIS MARTINSON
December 12, 2013

—These birds fly outside the windows of thought: the history of modernity happened to everyone everywhere all at once. This fusion of comfort and Apocalypse. The angel leads his armies of light to certain victory. Yet his expression suggests reluctance, as if he had wanted to postpone the battle a while longer—he has more armor to put on. A greave that fits his unprotected left leg leans against an oak tree. History comes to us through unguarded speech and spontaneous thought. How are we to inhabit unsustainable durations while listening to sworn testimony? [I.3; II.4; III.1a–1b; IV.3; V.1]

I.3; Epigraph 3: What matters in poetry is only the understanding that brings it about. (Osip Mandelstam)

II.4; Chapter 4: "The Invasion of Cambodia on Crane's Beach, May 1, 1970"

III.1a–1b; Argument by antinomy: 1a. We are social all the way down; 1b. By far the greatest use of language is for thought and not communication, despite virtual dogma to the contrary. (Noam Chomsky)

IV.3; A trajectory of Western civilization's founding texts: 3. "The simple truth is this: during my first deployment, I was made to participate in things, the enormity of which is hard to describe. War crimes, crimes against humanity. Though I did not participate willingly, and made what I thought was my best effort to stop these events, there are some things that a person simply cannot come back from. I take some pride in that, actually." (Last letter of Daniel Somers, dated June 10, 2013)

V.1; The immediacy of Anagoge: 1. St. Michael in Trees.

FROM THE NOTEBOOKS OF TALLIS MARTINSON
November 4, 2010 (cont.)
(Copied as if from memory in Tallis's handwriting)

Narrative and Testimony of Sarah M. Grimké

Miss Grimké is a daughter of the late Judge Grimké, of the
Supreme Court of South Carolina, and sister of the late
Hon. Thomas S. Grimké.

"As I left my native state on account of slavery, and deserted
the home of my fathers to escape the sound of the lash
and the shrieks of tortured victims, I would gladly bury in
oblivion the recollection of those scenes with which I have
been familiar; but this may not, cannot be; they come over
my memory like gory spectres, and implore me with resist-
less power, in the name of a God of mercy, in the name of
a crucified Savior, in the name of humanity; for the sake of
the slaveholder, as well as the slave, to bear witness to the
horrors of the southern prison house. I feel impelled by a
sacred sense of duty, by my obligations to my country, by
sympathy for the bleeding victims of tyranny and lust, to
give my testimony respecting the system of American slavery,—to detail a few facts, most of which came under my
personal observation. And here I may premise, that the actors
in these tragedies were all men and women of the highest
respectability, and of the first families in South Carolina,
and, with one exception, citizens of Charleston; and that

their cruelties did not in the slightest degree affect their standing in society.

"A handsome mulatto woman, about 18 or 20 years of age, whose independent spirit could not brook the degradation of slavery, was in the habit of running away: for this offence she had been repeatedly sent by her master and mistress to be whipped by the keeper of the Charleston work-house. This had been done with such inhuman severity, as to lacerate her back in a most shocking manner; a finger could not be laid between the cuts. But the love of liberty was too strong to be annihilated by torture; and, as a last resort, she was whipped at several different times, and kept a close prisoner. A heavy iron collar, with three long prongs projecting from it, was placed round her neck, and a strong and sound front tooth was extracted, to serve as a mark to describe her, in case of escape. Her sufferings at this time were agonizing; she could lie in no position but on her back, which was sore from scourgings, as I can testify, from personal inspection, and her only place of rest was the floor, on a blanket. These outrages were committed in a family where the mistress daily read the scriptures, and assembled her children for family worship. She was accounted, and was really, so far as alms-giving was concerned, a charitable woman, and tender hearted to the poor; and yet this suffering slave, who was the seamstress of the family, was continually in her presence, sitting in her chamber to sew, or engaged in her other household work, with her lacerated and bleeding back, her mutilated mouth, and heavy iron collar, without, so far as appeared, exciting any feelings of compassion.

"A highly intelligent slave, who panted after freedom with ceaseless longings, made many attempts to get possession of himself. For every offence he was punished with extreme severity. At one time he was tied up by his hands to a tree, and whipped until his back was one gore of blood. To this terrible infliction he was subjected at intervals for several weeks, and kept heavily ironed while at his work. His master one day accused him of a fault, in the usual terms dictated by passion and arbitrary power; the man protested his innocence, but was not credited. He again repelled the charge with honest indignation. His master's temper rose almost to frenzy; and seizing a fork, he made a deadly plunge at the breast of the slave. The man being far his superior in strength, caught his arm, and dashed the weapon on the floor. His master grasped at his throat, but the slave disengaged himself, and rushed from the apartment. Having made his escape, he fled to the woods; and after wandering about for many months, living on roots and berries, and enduring every hardship, he was arrested and committed to jail. Here he lay for a considerable time, allowed scarcely food enough to sustain life, whipped in the most shocking manner, and confined in a cell so loathsome, that when his master visited him, he said the stench was enough to knock a man down. The filth had never been removed from the apartment since the poor creature had been immured in it. Although a black man, such had been the effect of starvation and suffering, that his master declared he hardly recognized him—his complexion was so yellow, and his hair, naturally thick and black, had become red and scanty; an infallible sign of long continued living on bad and insufficient food. Stripes, imprisonment, and the gnawings of hunger, had broken his lofty spirit for a season; and, to use his master's own exulting expression, he was "as humble as a dog." After a time he made another attempt to escape, and was absent so long, that a reward was offered for him, *dead or alive*. He eluded every attempt to take him, and his master, despairing of ever getting him again, offered to pardon him if he would return home. It is always understood that such intelligence will reach the runaway; and accordingly, at the entreaties of his wife and mother, the fugitive once more consented to return to his bitter bondage. I believe this was the last effort to obtain his liberty. His heart became touched with the power of the gospel; and the spirit which no inflictions could subdue, bowed at the cross of Jesus, and with the language on his lips—"the cup that my father hath given me, shall I not drink it?" submitted to the yoke of the oppressor, and wore his chains in unmurmuring patience till death released him. The master who perpetrated these wrongs upon his slave, was one of the most influential and honored citizens of South Carolina, and to his equals was bland, and courteous, and benevolent even to a proverb."

01:47

> MISSION INTELLIGENCE COORDINATOR: Looks kinda like blankets, they were praying, they had like . . .
>
> PILOT: JAG25 KIRK97 We get a good count, not yet?
>
> SENSOR OPERATOR: They're praying, they're praying. . . . This is definitely it, this is their force. Praying? I mean seriously, that's what they do.
>
> MISSION INTELLIGENCE COORDINATOR: They're gonna do something nefarious.

. . .

01:50

> MISSION INTELLIGENCE COORDINATOR: Adolescent near the rear of the SUV.
>
> SENSOR OPERATOR: Well, teenagers can fight.
>
> MISSION INTELLIGENCE COORDINATOR: Pick up a weapon and you're a combatant, it's how it works.

. . .

01:52

> SENSOR OPERATOR: One guy still praying at the front of the truck.
>
> PILOT: JAG25 KIRK97 Be advised, all pax [passengers] are finishing up praying and rallying up near all three vehicles at this time.
>
> SENSOR OPERATOR: Oh, sweet target. I'd try to go through the bed, put it right dead center of the bed.
>
> MISSION INTELLIGENCE COORDINATOR: Oh, that'd be perfect.

"There is another achievement of theirs about which we should hear. Even in the refectory they did not cease from mental prayer [*noera ergasia*: a concentratcd state of recollection in the depths of the heart. Elsewhere John Climacus says, "if you are careful to train your mind never to wander, it will stay by you even at mealtimes"] and by secret signs and gestures these holy men reminded each other of it. And they did this not only in the refectory, but everywhere they met or assembled.

"If one of them committed a fault, many of the brothers would seek his permission to take the matter to the shepherd and to accept both the responsibility and the punishment. When the great man found out that his disciples did this, he inflicted easier punishments, in the knowledge that the one punished was actually innocent. And he made no effort to discover the real culprit." (John Climacus)

"Morality will oppose politics in history and will have gone beyond the functions of prudence or the canons of the beautiful to proclaim itself unconditional and universal when the eschatology of messianic peace will have come to superpose itself upon the ontology of war. . . ."

(Emmanuel Levinas)

From the Notebooks of Tallis Martinson
November 3, 2010

—These figures in a landscape, moving into view through the sounds of a voice, resolve themselves into an idea of absolute violence. Its acceptance establishes "an order from which no one can keep their distance. Nothing is henceforth exterior." We identify ourselves with the victims and are moved by this as if by entertainment—a catharsis of self-pity and fear. These are our new territories of ecstasy. "The eschatological vision breaks with the totality of wars and empires in which one does not speak. It does not envisage the end of history within being understood as a totality but institutes a relation with the infinity of being which exceeds the totality. The first vision of eschatology (hereby distinguished from the revealed opinions of positive religions) reveals the very possibility of eschatology, that is, the breach of the totality, the possibility of a signification without a context." (Emmanuel Levinas)
[I.4; II.4; III.2a–2b; IV.2; V.2]

> I.4; Epigraph 4: 709. Hard winter; Duke Gottfried died. / 710. Hard year; crops failed. / 711. [blank spaces] / 712. Flood everywhere / 718. Charles devastated the Saxons with great destruction. (Annals of St. Gall)
>
> II.4; Chapter 4: "The Invasion of Cambodia on Crane's Beach, May 1, 1970"

III.2a–2b; Argument by antinomy: 2a. Order is derived from public assemblies of armed men. 2b. Every culture has an origin story that includes the end of the world. No one is ever found to be missing from a single one of these stories.

IV.1; A trajectory of Western civilization's founding texts: 1. Psalm 51: *Miserere mei, Deus*: Deliver me from bloodguiltiness . . . and my tongue shall sing aloud of thy righteousness.

V.3; The immediacy of Anagoge: 3. The Painted Word. This happiness in the immediacy of the world's end: there can be no end to the delight felt by every creature when the word and the thought become one.

CHAPTER 5

The Immediacy of Anagoge; Three Scenes from Sheep Meadow: 1. St. Michael in Trees; 2. St. Anthony's Gaze; 3. St. John on Patmos or, The Painted Word

FROM THE NOTEBOOKS OF TALLIS MARTINSON
June 22, 2013

—A duration of reciprocity in which to think my own thoughts and be truthful in my relation to others—a commonness of reference flung against the sky like birds. What would the true peace of equal justice feel like? Surely, in the coming century of drone strikes, I will be among the happy dead who will rejoice to be taught to speak again. [I.6; II.5; III.3a–3b; IV.2; V.1]

I.6; Epigraph 6: Daughter, From far away he visits you / like the true believer you have come to love / out of the river of yourself, not the Yalu / or the Mississippi. / Here his different eye—presence is the knowledge / that when you renew the world / all worlds will be renewed— / white water.

II.5; Chapter 5: "The Immediacy of Anagoge; Three Scenes from Sheep Meadow: 1. St. Michael in Trees; 2. St. Anthony's Gaze; 3. *St. John on Patmos* or, The Painted Word"

III.3a–3b; Argument by antinomy: 3a. The history we are living is being narrated to us as a military emergency in which the principle of order is itself at stake. Under such conditions, the technical violence of official power becomes unanswerable. Real violence becomes the incontrovertible self-evidence of the justice of power's argument. This is the romance of all authoritarianism. 3b. Fundamental change occurs when poets turn themselves into instruments for the metamorphosis—the withholding and unfolding—of literary time the rest of us have ceased to hear. "Poetry establishes itself with astonishing independence in a new extra-spatial field of action, not so much narrating as acting out in nature by means of its arsenal of devices, commonly known as tropes. The breach in the Papacy as a historical structure is envisaged in the *Commedia* and acted out insofar as the infinite raw material of poetic sound—which is inappropriately offered to culture as proper, which is ever distrustful and offensive to culture because of its suspiciousness, and which spits culture out like water used for gargling—is revealed and brought to light. There exists an intermediary activity between the act of listening and the act of speech delivery. This activity comes closest of all to performance and constitutes its heart, as it were. The unfilled interval between the act of listening and the act of speech delivery is absurd to its very core." (Osip Mandelstam)

IV.2; A trajectory of founding texts of Western Civilization: "Sonnet 77"

Thy glass will show thee how thy beauties wear,
Thy dial how thy precious minutes waste;
The vacant leaves thy mind's imprint will bear,
And of this book, this learning mayst thou taste.
The wrinkles which thy glass will truly show
Of mouthed graves will give thee memory;
Thou by thy dial's shady stealth mayst know
Time's thievish progress to eternity.
Look what thy memory cannot contain,
Commit to these waste blanks, and thou shalt find
Those children nursed, delivered from thy brain,
To take a new acquaintance of thy mind.
　　These offices, so oft as thou wilt look,
　　Shall profit thee and much enrich thy book.

V.2; The immediacy of Anagoge: 2. St. Anthony's Gaze: The harlot's beauty beyond temptation: all the practicalities of lust painted into the scene without diminishing desire's limitlessness by the breadth of a sparrow's wing. The sacking of the city in the background (the ordinary sounds of this carry this far) is a commonplace event and makes no difference to the soul's salvation or the saint's fierce joy. The angel of the Lord speaks to him: "I was here the whole time; I wanted to see you fight the demons in every place you watched and waited for me when you thought you were by yourself." In Sheep Meadow that afternoon I saw St. Michael going into battle at the head of his three armies, all his orders carried to every soldier's ear perfectly by the cries of children borne by the rushing winds bending the tops of the trees.

•

EDITOR'S NOTE (CRM) From my recent practice of my brother's method (October 2018)

Every citizen owes the state a life, our father, Justin Martinson (his father's abandoned son), announced to us, his sons, in 1968. On December 1, 1969, we as twins received in the nation's birthday draft lottery a number so low that we were sure to be drafted to serve in the Vietnam War. I now am able to agree with my father's harsh sentencing. But only if the American state pursues justice as its end, as its founding declaration promises—only if its everyday durations are justly ordered to secure the life, liberty, and pursuit of happiness of every human being understood as equal and infinitely valuable. Only if the following act of mutuality is made true by the ordinary performance and renewal of its words: "And for the support of this Declaration, we mutually pledge to each other our Lives, our Fortunes, and our sacred Honor." "Everyone in the room heard," Tallis told me in 2015, "what Sari's father said that night." Now I want to say to Tallis, in the midst of his silence: "In your notebooks you give access to another history—to the sound of reciprocity beneath the rhythms of our exterminatory complicity. Join yourself now to the living and detach yourself from the dead.

"What durations, within the family and within the state, will undo our deferential cowardice? Was our mother trying at the end to make it possible to register Sari's infinite value and therefore her own despite everyone's failure to reach out to Sari during all those years? 'Submitting history as a whole to judgment, exterior to the very wars that mark its end, the eschatological vision restores to each instant its full signification in that very instant: all the causes are ready to be heard.'" (Emmanuel Levinas)

From the Notebooks of Tallis Martinson
June 22, 2013 (cont.)
(In Tallis's handwriting, as if transcribed from memory)

"Testimony of Angelina Grimké Weld:

"Mrs. Weld is the youngest daughter of the late Judge Grimké, of the Supreme Court of South Carolina, and a sister of the late Hon. Thomas S. Grimké, of Charleston.

"FORT LEE, Bergen Co., New Jersey, Fourth month 6th, 1839.

"I sit down to comply with thy request, preferred in the name of the Executive Committee of the American Anti-Slavery Society. The responsibility laid upon me by such a request, leaves me no option. While I live, and slavery lives, I must testify against it. If I should hold my peace, 'the stone would cry out of the wall, and the beam out of the timber would answer it.' But though I feel a necessity upon me, and 'a woe unto me,' if I withhold my testimony, I give it with a heavy heart. My flesh crieth out, 'if it be possible, let this cup pass from me'; but, 'Father, thy will be done,' is, I trust, the breathing of my spirit. Oh, the slain of the daughter of my people! they lie in all the ways; their tears fall as the rain, and are their meat day and night; their blood runneth down like water; their plundered hearths are desolate; they weep for their husbands and children, because they are not; and the proud waves do continually go over them, while no eye pitieth, and no man careth for their souls."

02:41

> SENSOR OPERATOR: Well, sir, would you mind if I took
> a bathroom break real quick?
>
> PILOT: No, not at all, dude.
>
> . . .

03:17

> UNKNOWN: What's the master plan, fellas?
>
> PILOT: I don't know, hope we get to shoot the truck
> with all the dudes in it.
>
> SENSOR OPERATOR: Yeah.

[The Predator drone has only one missile on board—not enough to target three vehicles—so two Kiowa helicopters, known as "Bam Bam 41," are ordered to take up an attacking position. A plan is agreed: the helicopters will fire first, then the drone will finish the job by firing its Hellfire missile at the survivors.]

"In this monastery to which I have been referring, there was a man named Isidore, from Alexandria, who having belonged to the ruling class had become a monk. I met him there. The most holy shepherd, after having let him join, discovered that he was a troublemaker, cruel, sly, and haughty, but he shrewdly managed to outwit the cunning of the devils in him. 'If you have decided to accept the yoke of Christ,' he told Isidore, 'I want you first of all to learn obedience.'

'Most holy Father, I submit to you like iron to the blacksmith,' Isidore replied.

"The superior, availing of this metaphor, immediately gave exercise to the iron Isidore and said to him: 'Brother, this is what I want you to do. You are to stand at the gate of the monastery, and before everyone passing in or out you are to bend the knee and say, "Pray for me, Father, because I am an epileptic."' And Isidore obeyed, like an angel obeying the Lord.

"He spent seven years at the gate, and achieved deep humility and compunction.

"After the statutory* seven years [Note: It may be that the superior treated Isidore's haughtiness as fornication for which a seven years' penance was required by the Apostolic Canons] and after the wonderful steadfastness of the man, the superior deemed him fully worthy to be admitted to the ranks of the brethren and wanted to ordain him. Through others and also through my feeble intercession, Isidore begged the superior many times to let him finish his course. He hinted that his death, his call, was near, which in fact proved to be so. The superior allowed him to stay at his place, and ten days later, humbly, gloriously, he passed on to the Lord. A week after his death the porter of the monastery was also taken, for the blessed Isidore had said to him, 'If I have found favor in the sight of the Lord, you too will be inseparably joined to me within a short time.' That is exactly what happened, in testimony to his unashamed obedience and his marvelous humility.

"While he was still alive, I asked this great Isidore how he had occupied his mind while he was at the gate, and this memorable man did not conceal anything from me, for he wished to be of help. 'At first I judged that I have been sold into slavery for my sins,' he said. 'So I did penance with bitterness, great effort, and blood. After a year my heart was no longer full of grief, and I began to see how unworthy I was to live in a monastery, to encounter the fathers, to share in the divine Mysteries. I lost the courage to look anyone in the face, but lowering my eyes and lowering my thoughts even further, I asked with true sincerity for the prayers of those going in and out.'"

FROM THE NOTEBOOKS OF TALLIS MARTINSON
November 16, 2010

—In the actual event, other watchers of birds sat near me. Listening to the sparrow in the peopled quiet I heard voices.

In 1819, Audubon sold nine of his slaves. Among them may have been the "servant" who had once saved his life. Audubon never wrote of any of this in his journals. He called his desire to paint birds "almost a mania." Since early childhood, he wanted to possess them "with a frenzy beyond reason." "During my deepest troubles I frequently would wrench myself from the persons around me, and retire to some secluded part of our noble forests. . . . This never failed to bring me the most valuable of thoughts and always comfort, and, strange as it may seem . . . it was often necessary for me to exert my will, and compel myself to return to my fellow beings." He spoke of taking dictation directly from nature; he experienced transcendence in a wood thrush's call.

From Hieronymus Bosch's paintings I try to extract a vision of an actual bird (a dark-eyed junco or house sparrow for instance), his direct reports of Apocalypse notwithstanding. The young scribe's face is illuminated by happiness—his fluent pen flies. [I.1; II.5; III.3a–3b; IV.3; V.3]

I.1; Epigraph 1: As soon as thought dries up . . .

II.5; Chapter 5: "The Immediacy of Anagoge; Three Scenes from Sheep Meadow: 1. St. Michael in Trees; 2. St. Anthony's Gaze; 3. *St. John on Patmos* or, The Painted Word"

III.3a–3b; Argument by antinomy: 3a. The history we are living in the present is narrated to us as a military emergency . . . 3b. Historical change is produced by poets when they turn themselves into instruments of the metamorphosis—the withholding and unfolding—of *literary time* the rest of us have ceased to hear.

IV.3; A trajectory of founding texts of Western civilization: "The piles of heads disappear in the distance. I am diminished there . . ." (Osip Mandelstam)

V.3; The immediacy of Anagoge: 3. *St. John on Patmos* or, The Painted Word. This joy of the news John on Patmos brings from the angel directly to the page.

CHAPTER 6

You Must Not Blame Yourself

FROM THE NOTEBOOKS OF TALLIS MARTINSON
April 3, 2015

—Western literacy's fixed narrative point of view forces the deferment of justice until the end of history—this last moment. Until then, we victors—we beneficiaries—are off the hook—accidental enablers of a future perfection behind the back of our own actions in collusion with the state. Our innocence is criminal. In an age of finance, until historical justice is funded, we cannot pretend to be committed to democracy. We arrive at the limits of our historical self-knowledge without the immediacy of the presence of each other. The Spanish visitor will buy the triptych for his private chapel—these unmoored reveries from Sheep Meadow have lost touch with any original promise of a restored democratic commons of plenty derived from a costly victory over dearth. Will our senses be able to perform the work of a messianic eschatology just before the missiles strike? St. Michael at the head of

God's three armies: in the far distance the tiny merchant ship burns on the water, providing unintentionally the illumination of an actual event. This sound of wind in the trees as accompaniment for my burning mind. [I.5; II.4; III.1a–1b; IV.3; V.2]

> I.5; Epigraph 5: I am sorry that it has come to this. . . . You must not blame yourself. The simple truth is this: during my first deployment, I was made to participate in things, the enormity of which is hard to describe. War crimes, crimes against humanity. (Last Letter of Daniel Somers, dated June 10, 2013)
>
> II.4; Chapter 4: "The Invasion of Cambodia on Crane's Beach, May 1, 1970"
>
> III.1a–1b; Argument by antinomy: 1a. We are social all the way down. 1b. By far the greatest use of language is for thought and not communication, despite virtual dogma to the contrary.
>
> IV.3; A trajectory of founding texts of Western civilization: 3. "I am sorry that it has come to this. . . . Then, I pursued replacing destruction with creation. For a time, this provided a distraction, but it could not last. The fact is that any kind of ordinary life is an insult to those who died at my hand." (From the last letter of Daniel Somers dated June 10, 2013)
>
> V.2; The immediacy of Anagoge: 2. St. Anthony's Gaze: Everything is here; all gestures are meaningful. Every detail marks the unfolding of an unlimited

number of stories. Demons of the mind are active. Nothing written will save you. Demons in the trees are singing beautifully. Nothing will be lost.

In my practice I have found it useful to apply the third set of my *terza rima* of thought to this entry:

3.

a. The frayed scrim of continuity made from clichéd fragments of a national American exceptionalist triumphalism. (One of these is: "We the people.")

b. The intuition of an ecstatic history of the real possibility of universal reciprocity among equally valued lives implicit in the natural language faculty as a counternarrative to accounts of New World slavery motivated by its beneficiaries' perceived interests in minimizing the continuing enormities of its harms.

c. A new history of print-culture literacy as the anticipatory creation in the midst of material abundance of a nonmonetized duration of thought for the practice of unbounded reciprocity among equally valued lives.

"My new mistress proved to be all she appeared when I first met her at the door,—a woman of the kindest heart and finest feelings. She had never had a slave under her control previously to myself, and prior to her marriage she had been dependent upon her own industry for a living. She was by trade a weaver; and by constant application in a good degree preserved from the blighting and dehumanizing effects of slavery. I was utterly astonished at her goodness. . . . But, alas! This kind heart had but a short time to remain such. The fatal poison of irresponsible power was already in her hands, and soon commenced its infernal work. That cheerful eye, under the influence of slavery, soon became red with rage; that voice, made all of sweet accord, changed to one of harsh and horrid discord; and that angelic face gave place to that of a demon.

"Very soon after I went to live with Mr. And Mrs. Auld, she very kindly commenced to teach me the A, B, C. After I had learned this, she assisted me in learning to spell words of three or four letters. Just at this point of my progress, Mr. Auld found out what was going on, and at once forbade Mrs. Auld to instruct me further, telling her, among other things, that it was unlawful, as well as unsafe, to teach a slave to read." (Frederick Douglass)

"But it is not alone for the sake of my poor brothers and sisters in bonds, or for the cause of truth, and righteousness, and humanity, that I testify; the deep yearnings of affection for the mother that bore me, who is still a slaveholder, both in fact and in heart; for my brothers and sisters, (a large family circle) and for my numerous other slaveholding kindred in South Carolina, constrain me to speak: for even were slavery no curse to its victims, the exercise of arbitrary power works such fearful ruin upon the hearts of *slaveholders,* that I should feel impelled to labor and pray for its overthrow with my last energies and latest breath.

"I think it important to premise, that I have seen almost nothing of slavery on *plantations.* My testimony will have respect exclusively to the treatment of *"house-servants,"* and chiefly those belonging to the first families in the city of Charleston, both in the religious and in the fashionable world. And here let me say, that the treatment of *plantation* slaves cannot be fully known, except by the poor sufferers themselves, and their drivers and overseers. In a multitude of instances, even the master can know very little of the actual condition of his own field-slaves, and his wife and daughters far less. A few facts concerning my own family will show this. Our permanent residence was in Charleston; our country-seat (Bellemont) was 200 miles distant, in the north-western part of the state; where, for some years, our family spent a few months annually. Our *plantation* was three miles from this family mansion. There, all the field-slaves lived and worked. Occasionally, once a month, perhaps, some of the family would ride over to the plantation, but I never visited the *fields where the slaves were at work,* and knew almost nothing of their condition; but this I do know, that the overseers who had charge of them, were generally unprincipled and intemperate men. But I rejoice to know, that the general treatment of slaves in that region of country, was far milder than on the plantations in the lower country.

"Throughout all the eastern and middle portions of the state, the planters very rarely reside permanently on their plantations. They have almost invariably *two* residences, and spend less than half the year on their estates. Even while spending a few months on them, politics, field-sports, races, speculations, journeys, visits, company, literary pursuits, &c., absorb so much of their time, that they must, to a considerable extent, take the condition of their slaves on *trust,* from the reports of their overseers. I make this statement, because these slaveholders (the wealthier class), are, I believe, almost the only ones who visit the north with their families;— and northern opinions of slavery are based chiefly on their testimony.

"But not to dwell on preliminaries, I wish to record my testimony to the faithfulness and accuracy with which my beloved sister, Sarah M. Grimké, has, in her 'narrative and testimony,' on a preceding page, described the condition of the slaves, and the effect upon the hearts of slaveholders, (even the best) caused by the exercise of unlimited power over moral agents. Of the *particular acts* which she has stated, I have no personal knowledge, as they occurred before my remembrance; but of the spirit that prompted them, and that constantly displays itself in scenes of similar horror, the recollections of my childhood, and the effaceless imprint upon my riper years, with the breaking of my heart-strings, when, finding that I was powerless to shield the victims, I tore myself from my home and friends, and became an exile among strangers—all these throng around me as witnesses, and their testimony is graven on my memory with a pen of fire.

"Why I did not become totally hardened, under the daily operation of this system, God only knows; in deep solemnity and gratitude, I say, it was the *Lord's* doing, and marvellous in mine eyes. Even before my heart was touched with the love of Christ, I used to say, "Oh that I had the wings of a dove, that I might flee away and be at rest"; for I felt that there could be no rest for me in the midst of such outrages and pollutions. And yet I saw *nothing* of slavery in its most vulgar and repulsive forms. I saw it in the *city,* among the fashionable and the honorable, where it was garnished by refinement, and decked out for show. A few *facts* will unfold the state of society in the circle with which I was familiar, far better than any general assertions I can make."

03:48

> MISSION INTELLIGENCE COORDINATOR [speaking to the drone pilot about the helicopters]: . . . at ground force commander's orders we may have them come up, action those targets, and let you use your Hellfire for cleanup shot.
>
> PILOT: Kirk97, good copy on that, sounds good.
>
> . . .

04:01

> SENSOR OPERATOR: Sensor is in, let the party begin. . .

Tell you what, they could have had a whole fleet of Preds up here.

PILOT: Oh, dude.

. . .

04:06

PILOT: As far as a weapons attack brief goes, man, we're probably going to be chasing dudes scrambling in the open, uh, when it goes down, don't worry about any guidance from me or from JAGUAR, just follow what makes the most sense to you. Stay with whoever you think gives us the best chance to shoot, um, at them. And I'm with you on that. So I'll brief you up on the launch profile, we'll hit a weapons attack brief when we know what we're going to shoot.

. . .

HELIPCOPTERS: Kirk97, Bam Bam four-one has you loud and clear.

PILOT: OK, Bam Bam 41, Kirk97 have you loud and clear as well. Understand you are tracking our three vehicles, do you need a talk on or do you have them?

HELICOPTERS: 41 has them just south side of the pass of the reported grid, white Highland[er] followed by two SUVs.

PILOT: Kirk97, that's a good copy. Those are your three vehicles. Be advised we have about twenty-one MAMs [military-aged males], about three rifles so far PIDed in the group and, ah, these are your three.

· · ·

04:13

PILOT: It's a cool-looking shot.
SENSOR OPERATOR: Oh, awesome!

"There is an emerald to adorn the crown of this discourse, and I must not forget to tell of it. For on one occasion I initiated a discussion of stillness among the most experienced elders there. They smiled and in their own cheerful way they spoke to me courteously as follows: "Father John, we are corporeal beings and we lead a corporeal life. Knowing this, we choose to wage war according to the measure of our weakness, and we think it better to struggle with men who sometimes rage and are sometimes contrite than to do battle with demons who are always in a rage and always carrying arms against us.

"One of those memorable men showed me great love according to God. He was outspoken, and once, in his own kindly fashion, he said this to me: "Wise man, if you have consciously within you the power of him who said, 'I can do everything in Christ Who strengthens me' (Phil.4:13), if the holy Spirit has come upon you as on the Holy Virgin with the dew of purity, if the power of the Most High has cast the shadow of patience over you, then, like Christ our god, gird your loins with the towel of obedience, rise for the supper of stillness, wash the feet of your brethren in a spirit of contrition, and roll yourself under the feet of the brethren with humbled will. Place strict and unsleeping guards at the gateway of your heart. Practice inward stillness amid the twistings and the turbulence of your limbs. And, strangest of all perhaps, keep your soul undisturbed while tumult rages about you.

"Your tongue longs to jump into argument but restrain it. It is a tyrant, and you must fight it daily seventy times seven. Fix your mind to your soul as to the wood of a cross, strike it with alternating hammer blows like an anvil. It has to be mocked, abused, ridiculed, and wronged, though without in any way being crushed or broken; indeed it must keep calm and unstirred. Shed your will as if it were / some disgraceful garment, and having thus stripped yourself of it, go into the practice arena." (John Climacus)

04:22

SENSOR OPERATOR: PID [positive identification] weapons, I don't see any . . .

SAFETY OBSERVER: Got something shiny on the one at the right . . .

SENSOR OPERATOR: Right . . . That's weird . . .

PILOT: Can't tell what the [expletive] they're doing.

SENSOR OPERATOR: Probably wondering what happened.

SAFETY OBSERVER: There's one more to the left of the screen.

SENSOR OPERATOR: Yeah, I see them.

SAFETY OBSERVER: Are they wearing burqas?

SENSOR OPERATOR: That's what it looks like.

PILOT: They were all PIDed as males, though. No females in the group.

SENSOR OPERATOR: That guy looks like he's wearing jewelry and stuff like a girl, but he ain't . . . if he's a girl, he's a big one.

. . .

04:32

SAFETY OBSERVER: One of those guys up at the top left's moving.

SENSOR OPERATOR: Yeah, I see him. I thought I saw him moving earlier, but I don't know if he's . . . is he moving or is he twitching?

SAFETY OBSERVER: Eh, I think he moved. Not very much, but . . .

SENSOR OPERATOR: Can't, can't follow them both.

MISSION INTELLIGENCE COORDINATOR: There's one guy sitting down.

SENSOR OPERATOR [talking to individual on the ground]: What you playing with?

MISSION COORDINATOR: His bone.

. . .

04:33:

SENSOR OPERATOR: Oh, shit, Yeah, you can see some blood right there, next to the . . .

MISSION INTELLIGENCE COORDINATOR: Yeah, I seen that earlier.

. . .

04:36

> MISSION INTELLIGENCE COORDINATOR: Is that two? One guy's tending the other guy?
>
> SAFETY OBSERVER: Looks like it.
>
> SENSOR OPERATOR: Looks like it, yeah.
>
> MISSION INTELLIGENCE COORDINATOR: Self-aid buddy care to the rescue.
>
> SAFETY OBSERVER: I forget, how do you treat a sucking gut wound?
>
> SENSOR OPERATOR: Don't push it back in. Wrap it in a towel. That'll work.

. . .

04:38

> PILOT: They're trying to [expletive] surrender, right? I think.
>
> SENSOR OPERATOR: That's what it looks like to me.
>
> MISSION INTELLIGENCE COORDINATOR: Yeah, I think that's what they're doing.

. . .

04:40

> SENSOR OPERATOR: What are those? They were in the middle vehicle.
>
> MISSION INTELLIGENCE COORDINATOR: Women and children.
>
> SENSOR OPERATOR: Looks like a kid.
>
> SAFETY OBSERVER: Yeah, the one waving the flag.

. . .

04:42

SAFETY OBSERVER: I'd tell him they're waving their . . .

SENSOR OPERATOR: Yeah, at this point I wouldn't . . .
I personally wouldn't be comfortable shooting at
these people.

MISSION INTELLIGENCE COORDINATOR: No.

Tallis Martinson's Historical Method

(A Schematic Outline)

I. Seven Epigraphs

I.1. *As soon as thought dries up, it is replaced by words. A word is too easily transformed from a meaningful sign into a mere signal, and a group of words into an empty formula, bereft even of the sense such things have in magic. We begin to exchange set phrases, not noticing that all living meaning has gone from them. Poor, trembling creatures—we don't know what meaning is; it has vanished from the world. It will return only if and when people come to their senses and recall that we must answer for everything.* (Adapted from Nadezhda Mandelstam's *Hope Abandoned*)

I.2. *By far the greatest use of language is for thought and not communication, despite virtual dogma to the contrary.* (Noam Chomsky, from *What Kind of Creatures Are We?*)

I.3. *What matters in poetry is only the understanding that brings it about. Imagine something intelligible, grasped, wrested from obscurity, in a language voluntarily and willingly forgotten immediately after the act of intellection and realization is completed. The signal waves of meaning vanish, having completed their work; the more potent they are, the more yielding, and the less inclined to linger. . . . The quality of poetry is determined by the speed and decisiveness with which it embodies its schemes and commands in diction, the instrumentless, lexical, purely quantitative verbal matter. One must traverse the full width of a river crammed with Chinese junks moving simultaneously in various directions—this is how the meaning of poetic discourse is created. The meaning, its itinerary, cannot be reconstructed by interrogating the boatmen: they will not be able to tell how and why we were skipping from boat to boat. Poetry is not a part of nature, not even its best or choicest part, let alone a reflection of it—this would make a mockery of the axioms of identity; rather, poetry establishes itself with astonishing independence in a new extra-spatial field of action, not so much narrating as acting out in nature by means of its arsenal of devices, commonly known as tropes. . . .Contrary to our accepted way of thinking, poetic discourse is infinitely more raw, infinitely more unfinished than so-called "conversational" speech. Being raw material is precisely what brings it into contact with performing culture. . . .What is an image? An instrument in the metamorphosis of hybridized poetic discourse. Poets effect change by being the actual instruments in the metamorphosis of* literary time, *in the withholding and unfolding of literary time which we have ceased to hear but which we are taught is the narration of so-called "cultural structures." The usurpers of the Papal Throne could not but fear the sounds which Dante rained down on them, although they could be indifferent to the torture by instruments through which he betrayed them in heeding the laws of poetic metamorphosis. However, the breach in the Papacy as a historical structure is envisaged in the* Commedia *and acted out insofar as the infinite raw material of poetic sound—which is inappropriately offered to culture as proper, which is ever distrustful and offensive to culture because of its suspiciousness, and which spits culture out like water used for gargling—is revealed and brought to light. There exists an intermediary activity between the act of listening and the act of speech delivery. This activity comes closest of all to performance and constitutes its heart, as it were. The unfilled interval between the act of listening and the act of speech delivery is absurd to its very core. [Poetic] material is not [poetic] matter* (Osip Mandelstam, from "Conversation about Dante," and "Addenda to 'Conversation about Dante'")

I.4. *709. Hard winter; Duke Gottfried died.*

710. Hard year; crops failed.

711.

712. Flood everywhere

. . .

718. Charles devastated the Saxons with great destruction.

719.

720. *Charles fought against the Saxons.*

721. *Theudo drove the Saracens out of Aquitaine.*

722. *Great crops.*

723.

724.

725. *Saracens came for the first time.*

   (From the Annals of St. Gall)

I.5a. Until the entry of June 22, 2013:

   The piles of heads disappear in the distance;

   I am diminished there; no one will remember my
      name;

   but in the rustle of pages,

   and in the sound of children's games,

   I shall rise from the dead

   to say: "the sun!"

   (Osip Mandelstam, fragment from "Ode to Stalin")

I.5b. After June 22, 2013:

June 10, 2013

I am sorry that it has come to this.

*The fact is, for as long as I can remember my motivation for
getting up every day has been so that you would not have to
bury me. As things have continued to get worse, it has become
clear that this alone is not a sufficient reason to carry on. The
fact is, I am not getting better, I am not going to get better,
and I will most certainly deteriorate further as time goes on.
From a logical standpoint, it is better to simply end things*

quickly and let any repercussions from that play out in the short term than to drag things out into the long term.

You will perhaps be sad for a time, but over time you will forget and begin to carry on. Far better that than to inflict my growing misery upon you for years and decades to come, dragging you down with me. It is because I love you that I can not do this to you. You will come to see that it is a far better thing as one day after another passes during which you do not have to worry about me or even give me a second thought. You will find that your world is better without me in it.

I really have been trying to hang on, for more than a decade now. Each day has been a testament to the extent to which I cared, suffering unspeakable horror as quietly as possible so that you could feel as though I was still here for you. In truth, I was nothing more than a prop, filling space so that my absence would not be noted. In truth, I have already been absent for a long, long time. . . .

You must not blame yourself. The simple truth is this: During my first deployment, I was made to participate in things, the enormity of which is hard to describe. War crimes, crimes against humanity. Though I did not partici-pate willingly, and made what I thought was my best effort to stop these events, there are some things that a person simply can not come back from. I take some pride in that, actually, as to move on in life after being part of such a thing would be the mark of a sociopath in my mind. These things go far beyond what most are even aware of.

To force me to do these things and then participate in the ensuing coverup is more than any government has the right to demand. Then, the same government has turned around and abandoned me. They offer no help, and actively block the pursuit of gaining outside help via their corrupt agents at the DEA. Any blame rests with them. . . .

Since then, I have tried to fill the void. I tried to move into a position of greater power and influence to try and right some of the wrongs. I deployed again, where I put a huge emphasis on saving lives. The fact of the matter, though, is that any new lives saved do not replace those who were murdered. It is an exercise in futility.

Then, I pursued replacing destruction with creation. For a time this provided a distraction, but it could not last. The fact is that any kind of ordinary life is an insult to those who died at my hand. How can I possibly go around like everyone else while the widows and orphans I created continue to struggle? If they could see me sitting here in suburbia, in my comfortable home working on some music project they would be outraged, and rightfully so.

I thought perhaps I could make some headway with this film project, maybe even directly appealing to those I had wronged and exposing a greater truth, but that is also now being taken away from me. I fear that, just as with everything else that requires the involvement of people who can not understand by virtue of never having been there, it is going to fall apart as careers get in the way.

The last thought that has occurred to me is one of some kind of final mission. It is true that I have found that I am capable of finding some kind of reprieve by doing things that are worthwhile on the scale of life and death. While it is a nice thought to consider doing some good with my skills, experience, and killer instinct, the truth is that it isn't realistic. First, there are the logistics of financing and equipping my own operation, then there is the near certainty of a grisly death, international incidents, and being branded a terrorist in the media that would follow. What is really stopping me, though, is that I simply am too sick to be effective in the field anymore. That, too, has been taken from me.

Thus, I am left with basically nothing. Too trapped in a war to be at peace, too damaged to be at war. Abandoned by those who would take the easy route, and a liability to those who stick it out—and thus deserve better. So you see, not only am I better off dead, but the world is better without me in it.

This is what brought me to my actual final mission. Not suicide, but a mercy killing. I know how to kill, and I know how to do it so that there is no pain whatsoever. It was quick, and I did not suffer. And above all, now I am free. I feel no more pain. I have no more nightmares or flashbacks or hallucinations. I am no longer constantly depressed or afraid or worried.

I am free.

I ask that you be happy for me for that. It is perhaps the best break I could have hoped for. Please accept this and be glad for me.
(The last letter of Daniel Somers, dated June 10, 2013)

I.6. *Daughter,*
    From far away he visits you,
    A true believer,
    Whom you have come to love,
    Out of the river of yourself—and not the Yalu
    Or the Mississippi.
    Here, his different eye—
    Presence is the knowledge that when you renew the world
    All worlds will be renewed—
    White water.

I.7. *I remember as a child trying to love my grandfather and failing.* (Epigraph added to Tallis Martinson's historical method by his editor, Christopher Renthro Martinson)

II. Five Chapters

II.1 "Sworn Testimony Is Direct Evidence";

II.2 "On August 21, 1791, at the Age of Six, John James Audubon Dreams of Looking Up in Saint-Domingue in Couëron, France, near Nantes";

II.3 "On Burdick's Hill";

II.4 "The Invasion of Cambodia on Crane's Beach, May 1, 1970";

II.5 "The Immediacy of Anagoge; Three Scenes from Sheep Meadow: 1. St. Michael in Trees; 2. St. Anthony's Gaze; 3. *St. John on Patmos* or, The Painted Word"

III. Three Pairs of Antinomies

III.1a: We are social all the way down.

III.1b: By far the greatest use of language is for thought and not communication, despite virtual dogma to the contrary.

III.2a: Order is derived from public assemblies of armed men. The object of war is to secure the peace; the object of peace is to foresee war and to win it by every means.

III.2b: Every culture possesses origin stories that narrate the end of the world. No person, living or dead, is ever found to be missing from a single one of these stories.

III.3a: The history we are living is narrated to us as a state of historical emergency in which order itself is said to be under immediate threat. Given these conditions, we are led to believe that the violence of state power constitutes the self-evidence of its own legitimacy. Given the stakes, the appeal of empire to the right of self-defense encompasses the self-granting of quasi-legal permission to use essentially unlimited means of violent force—extending to torture, targeted assassination, and mass murder. Empire demands impunity as the sign, instrument, and self-evident legitimacy of the unlimited reach of its violence.

III.3b: Historical change occurs when poets turn themselves into instruments of the metamorphosis—the withholding and unfolding—of the *literary* time that the rest of us have ceased to hear but which nevertheless gets narrated to us as the foundation of "cultural structures." What matters in poetry is only the understanding that brings it about. The usurpers of the Papal Throne could not but fear the sounds which Dante rained down on them, although they could be indifferent to the torture by instruments through which he betrayed them in heeding the laws of poetic metamorphosis. However, the breach in the Papacy as a historical structure is envisaged in the *Commedia* and acted out insofar as the infinite raw material of poetic sound—which is inappropriately offered to culture as proper, which is ever distrustful and offensive to culture because of its suspiciousness, and which spits culture out like water used for gargling—is revealed and brought to light. There exists an intermediary activity between the act of listening and the act of speech delivery. This activity comes closest of all to performance and constitutes its heart, as it were. The unfilled interval between the act of listening and the act of speech delivery is absurd to its very core. [Poetic] material is not [poetic] matter.

IV. A Trajectory for Founding Texts of Western Civilization

IV.1: Psalm 51 (*Miserere mei*)
IV.2: Shakespeare, "Sonnet 77"

Sonnet LXXVII
William Shakespeare

Thy glass will show thee how thy beauties wear,
Thy dial how thy precious minutes waste:
The vacant leaves thy mind's imprint will bear,
And of this book this learning mayst thou taste.
The wrinkles which thy glass will truly show
Of mouthed graves will give thee memory;
Thou by thy dial's shady stealth may know
Time's thievish progress to eternity.
Look, what thy memory cannot contain
Commit to these waste blanks, and thou shalt find
Those children nurs'd, delivered from thy brain,
To take a new acquaintance of thy mind.

These offices, so oft as thou wilt look,
Shall profit thee and much enrich thy book.

IV.3a (Until June 22, 2013): The piles of heads disappear in the distance; / I am diminished there. / No one
will remember my name, / but in the rustle of pages and
the sound of children's games, / I shall return from the
dead / to say:"the sun!"

IV.3b (After June 22, 2013): The Last Letter of Daniel
Somers, dated June 10, 2013 ("I am sorry that it has come
to this")

V. The Immediacy of Anagoge;
Three Scenes from Sheep Meadow:

1. St. Michael in Trees; 2. St. Anthony's Gaze; 3. *St. John on
Patmos* or, The Painted Word
("St. Anthony's Gaze" and "The Painted Word" are
derived from two paintings by Hieronymus Bosch,
Triptych of the Temptation of St. Anthony and *St. John on
Patmos*, respectively.)

Ten Entries Arranged
for Meditative Practice

From the entry dated April 18, 2010:

—Every moment flows evenly toward a white field filled with commonplace thoughts and the sound of untranslated—suddenly untranslatable—speech. [I.4; II.2; III.1a–1b; IV.1; V.1

From the entry dated August 2, 2010:

—Sweet Lord: This hand toward her in the New World light: This destruction was not planned. I swear this by what I know. This mechanical revolution—this absence of help: Now this lust amid the screams of the heathen: This perfection of Grace lying behind what we did: I will guard admittance through its door: A lasting joy. A coyote lopes across a field bordered by stone walls that were made and abandoned years ago—the last time Englishmen pushed this far into the alien land. [I.5; II.2; III.2a–2b; IV.2; V.2]

From the entry of August 18, 2010:

—The November sun, this warmth of wind heard in the upper branches—against nature, as if the birds were speaking their enormous happiness in human tongue—untranslatable by anyone. Then, as we begin to hear it, we realize that it is the sound of helicopters' rotors that we have been waiting for all along—ever since we left Saigon. St. Michael in Trees. [I.6. II.2; III.3a–3b; IV.3; V.3]

From the entry of April 5, 2010:

—Lyrically—lightly—does it—St. Michael in Trees; St. Stephen getting even: The child shot by American soldiers from the helicopter after the journalists were killed: the left leg severed just below the knee: "This one will live." This question of knowledge; this question of fact; this question of act and its disclosure. [I.7; II.3; III.1a–1b; IV.1; V.1]

From the entry dated August 19, 2010:

—The wind when it comes will counsel caution and bring a plague. Your armies are scattered. Bright metal reflecting a child's perfect will and purpose. We caused this, and it happened: there will be no time soon in which to remember—no place from which to know the perfection of its logic as a sweetness of mind. [I.1; II.2; III.2a–2b; IV.1; V.3]   [I.1; II.3; III.2a–2b; IV.2; V.2]

From the entry dated November 4, 2010:

—A fall into history—this book of November reveries from gardens of earthly delight: a Puritan drone against the play of interpretations: a master narrative for the sake of lyrical presence—an opening onto absolute power. An

event—however inconsequential—has to imply a redemptive logic to be coherent—listening to birds without distraction, listing their sightings with a pencil in a battered
notebook; St. Michael in Trees—rumors of his promised
victory. [I.2; II.2; III.2a–2b; IV.2; V.1]   [I.2; II.3; III.3a–3b;
IV.3; V.3]

From the entry dated January 27, 2012:

—Print literacy's fixed narrative point of view enforces
the deferment of justice until some narrative end to all of
history. Until then, we victors are off the hook—accidental
enablers of perfection behind the back of our own actions
in collusion with the state—however criminal its official
acts formally may be judged to be at the end. By then we
will have learned to repent and achieve the reconciliation
necessary for final victory. [I.3; II.4; III.1a–1b; IV.1; V.1]

From the entry dated August 16, 2012:

—There is goodness too in history. It shouldn't be
so hard to find: this ability to create wealth out of flows
through the body—and flows of bodies—in time. Why
does love give way to the rage to possess beyond the limits of a just reciprocity? In the moment of thought we are
each other. Unlimited possession is also a lasting duration
we have made no provision to survive.

Our father, Justin, falsely gentle—a fierce child; our
father, against translation—believer in the immediacy of
the word, bringing his father home in his mind from France

in June of 1919 before a child has access to word-logic, *aetat* eighteen months: all the guns in Europe in both the infant and his father's failing thought. [I.4; II.4; III.2a–2b; IV.2; V.2]

From the entry dated March 2, 2015:

—No peace beyond the line. *Donna è gentil nel ciel che si compiange* [There is a blessed lady in heaven who feels such pity] / Haiti just above my head: These painted birds. [I.5; II.4; III.3a–3b; IV.3; V.3]

From the entry dated April 5, 2015 (The Notebooks' last entry):

—Birds at an angle of flight—something is falling there beneath them—inside a place of thought: St. Michael will lead God's armies of light—in what substance will his certain victory over every evil be made manifest? Oh, to be among his foot soldiers on that day! [I.6; II.5; III.1a–1b; IV.1; V.1]

Author's Note

Daybook from Sheep Meadow is a novel of linguistic dispersion that attempts to refract the lived immediacy of an American present of permanent war through a prism of historical justice. Its linguistic syntax tries to reflect accurately an interior consciousness deformed by a failed accommodation to the untold violence of a failing empire's exterminatory exploitation of Earth's limited resources. Language itself becomes a casualty when severed from the transcendence intrinsic to coherent narratives attuned to a universal general welfare of equally valued lives.

For this novel's form and content I have relied heavily upon the following works:

Robert C. Berwick and Noam Chomsky, *Why Only Us? Language and Evolution* (2016)

Peter Brown, *The Body and Society: Men, Women, and Sexual Renunciation in Early Christianity* (1988)

Grégoire Chamayou, *A Theory of the Drone* (2013)

John Climacus, *The Ladder of Divine Ascent* (ca. 600 CE)

Frederick Douglass, *Narrative of the Life of Frederick Douglass, an American Slave* (1845)

Emmanuel Levinas, *Totality and Infinity: An Essay on Exteriority* (1961)

Nadezhda Mandelstam, *Hope against Hope* (1970); *Hope Abandoned* (1974)

Osip Mandelstam, "Conversation about Dante" (1934); *The Voronezh Notebooks* (1936); "Ode to Stalin" (1935)

Robert Meister, *Justice Is an Option: A Democratic Theory of Finance for the Twenty-First Century* (2021)

Theodore Dwight Weld, ed., *American Slavery as It Is: The Testimony of a Thousand Voices* (1839)

Hayden White, *The Content of the Form: Narrative Discourse and Historical Representation* (1987)

Thank you all
for your support.
We do this for you,
and could not do
it without you.

DEEP
VELLUM

PARTNERS

pixel ||| texel

ADDITIONAL DONORS, CONT'D

Mark Haber
Mary Cline
Maynard Thomson
Michael Reklis
Mike Soto
Mokhtar Ramadan
Nikki & Dennis Gibson
Patrick Kukucka
Patrick Kutcher
Rev. Elizabeth & Neil Moseley
Richard Meyer

Scott & Katy Nimmons
Sherry Perry
Sydneyann Binion
Stephen Harding
Stephen Williamson
Susan Carp
Susan Ernst
Theater Jones
Tim Perttula
Tony Thomson

SUBSCRIBERS

Ned Russin
Michael Binkley
Michael Schneiderman
Aviya Kushner
Kenneth McClain
Eugenie Cha
Stephen Fuller
Joseph Rebella
Brian Matthew Kim
Anthony Brown

Michael Lighty
Ryan Todd
Erin Kubatzky
Shelby Vincent
Margaret Terwey
Ben Fountain
Caitlin Jans
Gina Rios
Alex Harris

FORTHCOMING FROM DEEP VELLUM

MIRCEA CĂRTĂRESCU · *Solenoid*

translated by Sean Cotter · ROMANIA

MATHILDE CLARK · *Lone Star*

translated by Martin Aitken · DENMARK

LOGEN CURE · *Welcome to Midland: Poems* · USA

CLAUDIA ULLOA DONOSO · *Little Bird*, translated by Lily Meyer · PERU/NORWAY

LEYLÂ ERBIL · *A Strange Woman*

translated by Nermin Menemencioğlu · TURKEY

FERNANDA GARCIA LAU · *Out of the Cage*

translated by Will Vanderhyden · ARGENTINA

ANNE GARRÉTA · *In/concrete*

translated by Emma Ramadan · FRANCE

JUNG YOUNG MOON · *Arriving in a Thick Fog*

translated by Mah Eunji and Jeffrey Karvonen · SOUTH KOREA

FISTON MWANZA MUJILA · *The Villain's Dance*, translated by Roland Glasser · *The River in the Belly: Selected Poems*, translated by Bret Maney · DEMOCRATIC REPUBLIC OF CONGO

LUDMILLA PETRUSHEVSKAYA · *Kidnapped: A Crime Story*, translated by Marian Schwartz · *The New Adventures of Helen: Magical Tales*, translated by Jane Bugaeva · RUSSIA

JULIE POOLE · *Bright Specimen: Poems from the Texas Herbarium* · USA

MANON STEFAN ROS · *The Blue Book of Nebo* · WALES

ETHAN RUTHERFORD · *Farthest South & Other Stories* · USA

BOB TRAMMELL · *The Origins of the Avant-Garde in Dallas & Other Stories* · USA